"You'll get into trouble that way someday."

Race drawled these words slowly, insolently.

"I . . . don't know what you mean," Jinx replied, flustered.

"You have this astonishing habit of sending out conflicting signals at one and the same time," he said, and grinned a wicked devil's grin.

She recoiled, startled by his perception. "I'm not sending any kind of signals, and if I were, they wouldn't be sent to *you*, Mr. Morgan."

Their eyes met, locked. He didn't touch her, but didn't need to. It was as if invisible hands were on her neck, lightly stroking from the lobes of her ears to the soft hollows above her collarbones.

"*Captain* Morgan," he whispered softly.
"Remember it, or the only signals being flown will be distress signals. From you."

Victoria Gordon, one of our leading authors from the "land down under," has charmed Harlequin Romance readers for several years with her humorous, engaging style. Her characterizations are evocative and her storylines always stimulating. Many of her books are set in the Australia she knows and loves.

Arafura Pirate

Victoria Gordon

Harlequin Books

TORONTO • NEW YORK • LONDON
AMSTERDAM • PARIS • SYDNEY • HAMBURG
STOCKHOLM • ATHENS • TOKYO • MILAN

Original hardcover edition published in 1989
by Mills & Boon Limited

ISBN 0-373-03025-8

Harlequin Romance first edition January 1990

To Stephanie

CHAPTER ONE

JINX BEAUMONT stood in silent fury, her blue eyes alight with rage as she chewed on her full bottom lip and tried to stare some hurry into the phalanx of Customs officers.

This snap security exercise, which had already delayed her by nearly fifteen minutes, looked like entombing her in the Darwin airport for another half-hour at least.

'And I'm already two days late,' she muttered, glowering yet again at the official, who returned her scowl with a cheerful, almost friendly grin.

Don't you smile at me, mate, she thought, doing her level best to stare him into some semblance of activity. Not an easy eask, since almost everyone in the line ahead was taller than her own five-foot-two, and any movement caused a breaking of eye contact.

And as they all shuffled forward with exasperating slowness, Jinx had already formulated the scenario for when she finally did reach the head of the line.

There would be the usual round of questions, the usual frustratingly slow invasion of baggage, the politely raised eyebrows, the jesting and the disbelief.

'And why have you come to Darwin, Miss . . . Beaumont?'

'Beaumont, yes. I've come to catch sharks.'

'Sharks?'

'That's what I said.'

Jinx continued the dialogue in her head, still some half-dozen people away from the actual confrontation and already angry.

She'd been this route before, and was certain she could

predict it almost word for word.

Next would come the sly grin, the half-hidden guffaw and more questions.

'You're here for the game fishing, then?'

'No, I'm here to catch sharks. I'm a scientist.'

'A scientist?' Then would come the long pause, the expectant pause as the Customs officer played his little trick of trying to get an explanation without asking.

In her fairer moments, Jinx wouldn't blame him. Such a conversation with a diminutive blonde wearing faded jeans, sandals and a T-shirt emblazoned with the slogan 'KISSING A SMOKER IS LIKE LICKING AN ASTRAY' could be enough to make the least hardened Customs officer a bit sceptical.

To be told that the blonde was, in fact, a doctor of marine sciences simply served to heighten the confustion.

'I should tell him I've just flown up for a dirty weekend with my boyfriend, who's a cop,' Jinx muttered to herself, her scowl deepening as the line slowed yet again. It was distinctly demeaning to have to spend precious minutes explaining that she was indeed a scientist, that she had come to Darwin—yet again—to spend the next month catching sharks, tagging them, and returning them to the sea. Especially, she thought, when she'd said it all before on a previous visit.

'I wonder if they put on these little security exercises just for me,' she muttered, and found the comment drawing curious glances from the two women immediately ahead of her in the line. They looked away at her fierce scowl, but stayed curious.

Then, surprisingly, the queue began to move with a semblance of life, and Jinx, her lines fully rehearsed, found herself before the same Customs officer she'd had to face on that previous occasion. The man she'd been scowling at had somehow disappeared.

'Sharks again, I suppose,' he said with a slow grin, and she couldn't help but respond.

The scowl was transformed as her own smile revealed white, even teeth, and her blue eyes danced with the delight of having been remembered.

'You'll be thinking we put on these exercises just for you,' the man said, his grin widening as his eyes traced the slogan across the front of her T-shirt. Not missing what was under the T-shirt either, Jinx noticed.

'I had been wondering that,' she admitted. 'Especially this trip, because I'm two days late already and I'm afraid the skipper'll be chopping me up for bait.'

A blatant lie, that one. Will Jacobs might fume a little at the delays, but would never be anything but kindess itself where Jinx was concerned. He treated her at worst like a wayward granddaughter, and his gruff, risqué bantering was laughingly reciprocated.

'Well, it certainly wouldn't be proper to make you go through all this nonsense again if you're running late, Dr Beaumont,' the Customs officer said—rather to Jinx's surprise, because the look in his eye made it abundantly clear that he'd like nothing better than to renew acquaintanceship. She remembered that on the previous occasion he'd ended by offering a dinner invitation, and she half expected that again, as well.

Especially considering he'd remembered her name without prompting. And her doctorate. She smiled back at him, feeling qite delighted by it all despite her delays.

'I wouldn't mind if it happened on my way back to Hobart,' she replied. 'Then, I've usually got plenty of time, but coming this way I always seem to be running late, for some reason.'

'I'll try and arrange that,' the Customs officer said, and would, Jinx was certain, have followed up with another request for a date. She didn't give him a chance.

'You do that. I should be going in about a month,' she said, hastily gathering her belongings. 'But now I'd better be off to Stoke's Hill wharf, or I'll be in more trouble than I can handle.'

She emerged into the airport proper to find—thank heaven—Bronwyn Davis pacing anxiously back and forth with a worried look on her face.

The tall, angular redhead was Jinx's liaison with the Northern Territory fisheries branch, and it was a mark of their mutual respect that Bronwyn had come herself instead of sending some minion to drive Jinx to the waiting boat.

'Don't say it; I know. Late as usual,' Jinx said as the redhead smiled a welcome. 'But it isn't my fault, not this time.'

Nor was it. The two-day delay had been caused by her chief at the Commonwealth Laboratories in Hobart demanding a complete redraft of a particularly involved research report.

Not that the redraft had improved anything. If anything, Jinx thought, the rewrite had only added to existing confusion by exchanging her own precise wording for the convoluted style common to most scientific papers. Nor had the speed helped. She had pushed herself to the limit getting the work done, which meant starting on the long series of flights to Darwin with virtually no sleep and her packing little more than a shambles.

I suppose I might as well get used to going without sleep, she'd told herself between unsatisfactory naps on the various aircraft that carried her north. Her month aboard the *Perfidy*, she knew from past experience, would allow precious little time for mundane habits like sleeping. Weather permitting, the small scientific crew under her leadership would work any and all hours in their bid to gather as much information as possible during the limited time available to them.

It meant being up before dawn, working through until midnight or later, with only hastily snatched meals and the occasional catnap on deck, and getting up early the next morning to do it all again.

Hard work, not improved by the total lack of privacy, the crowdedness of eight people jammed into a boat designed for three or four. But satisfying.

Infinitely more satisfying, she thought, than the drudgery of her day-to-day work in Hobart, where she was forced to work inside, collating statistics and trudging through mazes of detail and the intricacies of scientific reports.

Once outside the airport, Jinx drew in deep breaths of the hot, humid, typically-Darwin air and felt her skin prickle immediately to the tropic temperatures. What a splendid change from Hobart in June, she thought, remembering that Mount Wellington had been crowned with snow when she'd left. Here it was scarcely breakfast time, but already the temperature was soaring.

It would be in the thirties by midday; temperatures that would have Tasmanians screaming about heatwaves and rushing for the nearest beaches, yet to Darwin residents it was mid-winter and she would find some of them dressed accordingly in thick jumpers.

Bronwyn navigated her little red Datsun through Darwin's traffic with frightening speed and skill, but Jinx hardly noticed in her pleasure at being back. It was a city she had fallen in love with on her very first visit three years before, and time had only enhanced the relationship.

She had never seen Darwin before the devastation of Cyclone Tracy in 1974, when Christmas morning saw much of the town destroyed. But the new, modern

Darwin, growing with a vitality typical of Australia's Northern Territory, was very much to her taste.

There wasn't time to see much of it this trip, however. They sped through to the harbour and the waiting bulk of the *Perfidy*, a seventy-foot gill-netter that hovered beside the wharf on long springers to cope with Darwin's large tidal fluctuation.

Jinx grabbed up her gear, shouted a goodbye to Bronwyn, and trotted eagerly towards the boat that would be her home for the next month or more.

Cries of welcome came from the foredeck, and she looked up to see the familiar face of Brian Roberts, who'd been part of her scientific crew on her last voyage aboard the *Perfidy*.

'Jinx and Judas and Jonah!' he cried, rushing to help bring her gear aboard. 'I wish they'd told me it would be you; I'd have taken on some other project. I don't think I could stand another solid month of being seasick.'

Jinx didn't immediately reply. Her reputation as a bringer of bad weather, while not surprising considering her father's ridiculous choice of names for his firstborn daughter, was not something she appreciated.

Especially as it proved true all too often. The last trip had been a nightmare of squalls and cyclone weather. Everybody on board but the skipper and herself had been thoroughly seasick with monotonous regularity— especially, she thought with despair, young Brian—and while she'd copped the blame in good spirit, there was always that niggling feeling that perhaps she *was* a jinx, some sort of marine hoodoo.

'I can't help it if the weather gets strange when I'm at sea,' she said to Brian. 'And it isn't my fault if you insist on being seasick all the time, either. You really should have sorted that out before you decided to get into marine biology.'

'Too late now,' was the grinning reply. Brian was a
tall, lanky redhead with a boyish attitude that Jinx had
sometimes found a bit much to take. He was fun, could be
charming when it pleased him, but most often fell into the
role of fumble-fingered teenager despite the fact he was
only a year off his own doctorate and well past twenty-
one.

'Where's everybody else?' she asked, mildly surprised
to see none of the crew aboard. In fact, the *Perfidy*
appeared to be deserted but for Brian and herself.

'Skipper's sulking in his cabin. Crew's getting last-
minute supplies and our lot's off playing tourist.'

'Playing tourist? But surely you all knew I was arriving
this morning? I'd expected we'd be at sea within an
hour,' Jinx queried.

'Not my hassle,' Brian replied evasively, and with just
enough of something in his voice that she threw him a
quick glance, immediately wondering what he'd been up
to, why he was on board while the rest of her crew were
out enjoying themselves.

Well, it didn't matter. If the boat's crew were also
ashore, it would be with the skipper's approval, and if
they didn't ship out this morning, it wouldn't mean the
end of the world, Jinx thought.

Then Brian's earlier comment registered. Will Jacobs
sulking in his cabin? That just didn't ring true. Old Will
had never, to Jinx's knowledge, ever sulked in his life. He
was a hard-drinking, hard-working fishing captain of the
old school, living a life of lusty pleasure that didn't
acknowledge such civilised activities as sulking.

Unless some woman had done him in, she thought. Not
an impossible suggestion at all; he was notorious for his
romantic adventures and—from all she'd heard on
previous voyages—justifiably so.

'I'd better check in with the skipper,' she said, putting

words to her thought. 'He's probably blaming me for holding things up as it is.'

Leaving Brian to whatever he'd been about when she'd arrived, she found her way to the door that led to the skipper's cabin, knocked briefly, then flung open the door and rushed in with a loud shout.

'Come out and fight, you old . . .' The cry died, throttled in her very throat by the sight of the figure that had turned in his chair to stare at her.

Eyes like the palest of tropical green seas burned from a tanned face so ruggedly featured it might have been chiselled from stone. Roughly. It was *not* Will Jacobs!

His hair was short-cropped, black as night except for a dusting of grey that gave it a salt-and-pepper look, and that hair was coarse as steel wire. Strong brows beetled over those incredible eyes, and his nose was high-bridged about a mouth that promised cruelty or intense sexuality. Or both. His chin was firm, determined, and the lines through the mahogany of his skin promised strength of character beyond anything she'd ever seen.

A pirate, was Jinx's first impression.

He didn't rise, just sprawled in the chair with the careless poise of some great hunting cat at rest. Only his eyes moved, at first, roaming over her with maddening insolence. They scanned the message on her T-shirt, touching her breasts like a caress. Then he reached across to shake out a cigarette from the pack on the table, lit it, and blew the smoke out through his flaring nostrils in a gesture that could be nothing but contemptuous.

Jinx could only stand her ground. She'd gone too far to retreat, too far to continue in the face of this piratical stranger. She stood there, enduring his stares and trying to face him down, despite the certain knowledge that she was doomed to failure.

His eyes were those of a predator: icy, merciless and

totally without evidence of the character of the person behind them. The devil would have eys like that, Jinx found herself thinking.

Again, he blew smoke through his nostrils, then spoke in a voice that matched the rest of him. It was rough, growling, deep, and powerful. It matched the strength of his features too well for her taste.

'If your T-shirt means anything, you haven't come to kiss me,' he said with a slight quirk of sensuous lips. 'But you obviously reckon you've got some business here, so I guess I'm supposed to say, Dr Beaumont, I presume? And two days late in the bargain.'

'Unfortunately, yes,' Jinx began, only to have him interrupt as if she hadn't even begun to speak.

'Two days in which your boffins have played merry hell with my boat, that young hoon on the foredeck has caused me not inconsiderable inconvenience just to keep him out of jail, and all you can say is ''unfortunately''?'

'You haven't given me a chance to say much else,' Jinx replied defensively.

He leaned back in the chair, muscular arms folded across an equally muscular chest. The deep, salt-water tan against the sparkling white of his own T-shirt and shorts—his only garments—made him look as if he'd been carved from teak, or perhaps mahogany.

'I . . . I don't know what to say,' she was forced to admit—and took no pleasure at all in the glimmer of satisfaction she saw in his eyes.

Smug, self-righteous bastard! she thought, and found her temper beginning to roil at the attitude of this infuriating stranger.

When he didn't reply, she forced herself to be more positive, to demand.

'And before I say anything at all, you might at least do me the courtesy of introducing yourself. As well as explaining what you're doing in Captain Jacobs' cabin, just for starters.'

His grin was shark-false, wolf-wise. It never touched his eyes, and his eyes never stopped touching her body through the thin material of the T-shirt.

'Race Morgan,' he replied bluntly, then added, quite unnecessarily, 'Captain Race Morgan to you.'

Jinx felt her stomach lurch. She should have known! Known, or at the very least suspected. Race Morgan owned the entire fleet from which the *Perfidy* was chartered for government work. He was almost a Darwin legend, at least in the fishing industry, for having parlayed a clapped-out trawler into a world-class fishing fleet before he was thirty. An age, she thought irreverently, he wouldn't see again.

Even as she stared at him, mesmerised by those pale green eyes, she found her memory spitting forth small bits of data it had picked up since her first trip to Darwin.

Morgan would be. . . nearer forty now, she thought. Renowned throughout his industry as an innovator, a mover and a shaker, a cut-throat businessman and yet a man known for strange, inexplicable gestures of softness.

She knew—having heard it from the man involved—that he'd once given one of his boats to a fisherman whose own boat had been sunk in an accident that was never satisfactorily explained.

'The powers that be did their best to write me off,' the fisherman had told her. 'They wanted my guts, they did. But Morgan, he didn't so much as ask a question. He just gave me the *Seahorse* and told me to give it back when I was flush again, or buy it if I liked. Never a word about rent or compensation or any other bloody thing.'

The fisherman had nearly been in tears by the time he'd finished his story, but the overall impression had been firm as if set in concrete. He was Race Morgan's man from that day forward, and proud of it.

Morgan's reputation as a womaniser was no less vivid. He was reputed to have left children in every Australian fishing port from Darwin south, but Jinx had no personal knowledge of the truth of that.

Just as well, she thought. Because it would be only too easy to believe such tales of this dark, ice-eyed figure. Race Morgan, like his legendary namesake, was every inch a pirate. She felt his approach to life, work and women would be all the same, the swaggering cut-throat approach of a true buccaneer.

She found herself giving her head a brief shake to bring back the present, and realised she'd been drifting into thought at the expense of keeping Race Morgan under careful scrutiny.

He was no longer in the captain's chair, but stood only inches from her, staring down from a considerable height. He would have to be eight inches taller than Jinx, and when not in repose his muscular figure was even more predatory than first impressions suggested.

'Do you always go off in a trance like that when you're talking to people?' he said, and at such close range that rumbling voice was like a volcano about to explode.

'No, I don't, actually,' Jinx replied, fighting off the urge to retreat, the feeling that he was too close, that he had only to reach out and take her. And he would . . . could.

'What's happened to Captain Jacobs?' she asked quickly, not entirely sure she wanted the answer, but knowing she must have it. Could it be that this man would be skipper for the coming voyage? Best not, thank you very much.

'In hospital.' Her worst fears confirmed. 'He had a mild heart attack three days ago, and right at the moment is doing well enough to hold his own, although I doubt he'll be back in this cabin very soon.'

'So who's . . .' She paused. There was no need to ask; the look in his eye carried the message only too clearly.

'If you want to go and visit him, there'll be time,' Race Morgan was, astonishingly, saying. 'He'd like it, for sure. I know he thought a great deal of you.'

Jinx didn't know what to reply. The suggestion had been made in his normal voice, but somehow the rumbling fierceness had been transformed into something . . . gentle?

'I'd like that,' she said. 'If he's well enough, that is. I shouldn't want to complicate things.'

'He'd thrive on it.'

Then he did something even more surprising. Stepping back to his desk, he rummaged in a drawer and then tossed a jingling ring of keys which Jinx only barely caught.

'My vehicle's the red Pajero,' he said. 'We won't be shipping out before tomorrow morning now, so take all the time you want today with Will. If you get back in time for tea, it'll be soon enough for me.'

'Oh, but . . . well, wouldn't I be better to take a cab?' she asked. 'You might need your vehicle, or—well, whatever. I just wouldn't feel right taking it.'

'It'll be all right,' he said with a slow, surprisingly warm smile. 'I'm not going anywhere this afternoon, and when the crew get back we'll have vehicles enough to dispose of.'

Once again his eyes roved across her body, but now the arrogance had softened, somehow. Now his assessment was of Jinx as a woman, not simply as prey. She didn't know which was worse; this survey seemed somehow even more intimate than his undisguised lust earlier.

'And if you're going, best hop to it,' he said, voice alive with the interest she could see in his eyes. 'Or I might decide to let you test your beliefs.'

'*Let* me?' The challenge couldn't be met, but it couldn't be ignored either. Jinx had been fighting her way through a man's world all her working life, and felt at least reasonably capable of taking care of herself.

Her mouth quirked as she focused her bright blue eyes on Race Morgan, and subconsciously she stretched to the full potential of her diminutive height.

'You're trying to suggest you've already tested it?' he said with a suggestive grin. 'I suppose you may have, but generalisation is bad for the soul, in case you haven't realised that yet. You can make some shocking mistakes by generalising.'

'I could say the same to you,' Jinx replied. 'I realise many women would be impressed by your super-macho approach, but it would be a mistake for you to think all women are alike.'

'One mistake I would never make,' was the reply. 'It's because they're so definitely *not* alike that I'm attracted to them in the first place.'

And with a pantherish stride he was in front of her, his hands like iron bands at her waist. Jinx didn't have time to object before his lips descended.

His kiss was harsh, at first. She could feel only the strength of him, the texture of his lips, the held-in savagery of his kiss. Her struggle against him was futile; short of kneeing him in the groin, which she was loath do do, she simply had no defences.

Then his tongue was parting her lips, and she became aware of the taste of him, the scent of his after-shave wafted into her nostrils, and his hands at her waist seemed less iron bands and more—far more—human hands.

Her own response was unexpected. She was unready for it, therefore, and less able to muster an opposition. It seemed to grow like a vast wave inside her, rising to flood her body with warmth, to waken all her senses.

He didn't taste like an ashtray; he didn't even taste of
the cigarette she'd watched him smoke. And his touch at
her waist was now light, almost a caress, yet she felt as if
she was more chained than before.

The heat of his body flowed through the thin T-shirts
that separated them, and the male strength of him was
rigid against the softness of her tummy, its power flowing
to help ignite the fire that now burned through her. His
every touch seemed to sensitise her to him, and she was
afraid.

Afraid? No, that wasn't the proper word. Terrified
would be better, because now his hands were moving
along the length of her back, tracing intimate designs
along the nubbles of her spine. And each touch seemed to
create a new and more delicious response, a response her
conscious mind recognised as dangerous.

Her own arms had somehow lifted to clasp themselves
around his neck, and now they too seemed to become
quite independent of her mind's instructions. Instead of
clawing at him, her fingers had begun to wander down
along the muscles of his shoulders, and her lips had
softened, the better to accept his kiss.

This is insane! Her mind screamed the accusation, but
her body was past listening. The touch of fingers beneath
her T-shirt, playing at the softness of her waistband,
insisting on a response, demanding a response.

And getting one. Whereupon his kiss ended without
any warning whatsoever.

It was a brutal act. And he knew it too. Race Morgan's
icy eyes glimmered with satisfaction as he stared down
into blue-grey eyes now softened by accepted
vulnerability.

His voice was soft, but cruel.

'I've got an ashtray, if you'd care for a bit of

comparison shopping,' he said—and caught her flailing hand as it rose to swing at his face.

'You . . . bastard!'

'My mother wouldn't agrée.'

'Damn you . . .' She stopped. His eyes stopped her, without even the help of his grip at her waist. No, she couldn't say that—not to this man. 'Let me go!'

'Only if you promise to stop trying to smack me. Don't you know that violence is only the last resort of the incompetent?'

'A very satisfying last resort,' Jinx muttered, feeling the violence drain away from her. It was hard to meet his eyes now; harder still to accept her defeat gracefully.

And yet she must. Now that her mind was freed of the temptation of his kisses, his caresses, she knew that if she didn't sort this situation out it would make the next month unbearable, unendurable.

'I think I'll go now,' she said, wriggling her waist free of his grip. He didn't argue, didn't attempt to stop her. Just that shark-grin of satisfaction.

'Drive carefully.' His voice drifted out of the cabin behind her, flowed like a shadow behind her as she negotiated the narrow stairwell down to the main deck.

Brian looked up expectantly from his place on the foredeck, then his eyes dropped just as quickly as he sensed her mood.

Whatever he'd done—and she'd have to find out sooner or later, Jinx realised—it had been serious to keep Brian so subdued. Normally he'd relish the opportunity to catch her so vulnerable, but now he was playing coy, and that, somehow, worried her even more.

Grabbing up her gear, unwilling to even glance back to where she knew Race Morgan would be watching, she made her way down the companionway to the fo'c'sle, which she would share with the boat's crew and her own party throughout the voyage.

It took only moments to stow away the few bits of clothing she'd brought with her. T-shirts, shorts, half a dozen brief swimsuits, and several pairs of jeans comprised virtually all of it. Except for the one cocktail dress that was packed separately with its accessories in a hanger-bag.

Race Morgan was nowhere to be seen when she emerged a few minutes later, changed into a less provocative T-shirt and a pair of brief shorts.

Just as well, Jinx thought, then wondered what difference it could possibly make. They'd had their confrontation and he'd won—just as he'd expected to win. The best thing she could do now was to try and forget it, along with doing her best to ensure there was no repeat performance.

She found Morgan's Pajero, which she drove with exceptional care despite an inner urge to run it off the end of the wharf, and reached the hospital just in time to find Will Jacobs berating a rather comely, no-longer-young nurse for being so unswervingly firm with him.

'I might as well be dead as have to live by following all your bloody orders, young woman!' he was shouting in a voice Jinx could hear from way down the hall. 'What's the sense of being alive if you take all the fun out of it?'

His shouted greeting to Jinx did nothing to improve his credit with the nursing Sister, who shot Jinx a filthy look when Will demanded that she 'take off your clothes and stay awhile. Be a pleasant change after this old hen.'

'You're nothing but a dirty old man; I'm surprised they don't wash out your mouth with soap three times a day,' Jinx replied with a warm grin.

She leaned over to kiss him, marvelling at how he could look so healthy only days after a heart attack. On appearances, he should be back on his boat, not lying in a hospital bed and making a nuisance of himself, she thought.

Then she looked into his eyes and revised her opinion. The pain was still there, and the weakness with it, no matter how much he pretended otherwise. He'd seen death close enough to shake hands with, and behind the bluster and bravado was fear.

'You might have told me you were going crook; I might have come earlier,' she joked, forcing lightness into her voice. Will didn't need gloom and doom, now now. He needed to have his bluster accepted, needed to feel that he was still able to charm the girls, that he'd be walking out of this hospital whenever he was ready.

'It's not much. I'll be getting out of here sooner than you think,' he said as if reading her thoughts. 'Wasn't for interfering damned biddies like Sister Watson here, I'd be out already.'

Jinx glanced from the nursing Sister to the patient, quick to sense the feelings beneath the apparent antagonism. Maybe he was right, she thought, gladdened to see that Will had maintained his virile approach so well in the face of such adversity.

But then she caught a flicker of something else from Sister Watson and was less sure. It was obvious the two antagonists were old friends, perhaps even old lovers, and Sister Watson wasn't pleased with the older man's progress.

'You're not to stay long,' she told Jinx, and her eyes stressed the significance. 'He's not as tough as he thinks he is, old Will, and I want him resting, not getting all excited.'

'Only because you're too old and fat to excite me,' the old man growled, his tone rough but still revealing an undeniable affection for the nurse. As she left the room, he winked at Jinx, who returned the wink with a frown.

'You're absolutely incorrigible,' she said. 'And it isn't anything to be one bit proud of.'

'Pride isn't the most important thing at my age,' he replied impudently, then sank back against his pillow with a deep sigh.

'Well, staying alive ought to be, and you won't manage that by insisting on being a silly old twit,' Jinx replied.

From her very first meeting with the old man she had instinctively known that she could only survive by matching his incredible zest for life. She had traded bawdy jest with bawdy jest, accepted his insistence that he was only just waiting for her to grow up before asserting his masculine dominance. It had given them a comfortable relationship, harmlessly boosting both their egos without any threat to either, and their joking, teasing relationship had made earlier voyages good fun for all the crew.

But now? Now Jinx wasn't sure she could maintain the façade. She was worried by the pain in Will's eyes, by the fear he so desperately tried to hide.

'It's not real good, is it?' she said, meeting his eyes, trying to absorb some of the pain, to give him any measure of relief.

'It could be worse. I could be a goner,' he replied gruffly. 'Damn near fell overboard when it hit me; would have if Race hadn't been there. He caught me by the back of me stubbies and near gave me a squeaky voice for ever.'

Jinx laughed out loud at the mental picture, but her laughter died too quickly. It was the face of Race Morgan that killed it; she had trouble seeing him as anything but a plunderer, despite knowledge to the contrary.

And, sick as he was, Will Jacobs caught it.

'You've met the big skipper, then,' he said, and didn't even try to make it a question. 'And you didn't go much on him, which hardly surprises me.'

'I didn't melt the first time he looked at me, if that's what you mean,' Jinx replied. 'Which I suppose is what you expected—*he* certainly seemed to.'

'You wouldn't have been the first,' the old man replied with a ghost of a smile. 'But of course, being *you*, you more likely kicked him in the cobblers instead, just to show him you weren't interested.'

Jinx giggled at the thought, then remembered that she *had* thought of it, however fleetingly.

'I did not!' she scoffed. 'And I'd have to be almost as old as you, and male to boot, not to be interested.'

'Good.'

The old man's voice was getting weaker, and Jinx decided it was time to end both speculation and visit.

'Not good,' she replied. 'And not to be discussed any more. You may be able to handle Sister Watson, but I certainly couldn't. And don't intend to try. Instead I'm going off to play tourist for a bit, then get back to the ship with the skipper's vehicle before he thinks I've stolen it or something.'

She leaned down to kiss him lightly on the forehead. 'And you're going to rest and be well so I can expect to see you waving from the dock when we come back. OK?'

'It might be if this place wasn't so damned boring,' with the sullen reply. 'I don't suppose you'd arrange to smuggle me in some grog before you ship out?'

'Certainly not!'

Jinx's cry was echoed by one from the open doorway, and she turned to see Sister Watson with an expression of horror that matched her own.

'Don't worry, Sister. I meant exactly what we both said,' Jinx said sternly. 'And I'll make damned sure nobody else from the boat tries anything so stupid, either.'

'It's already been tried. And failed.' Will's voice was cranky, showing not the slightest remorse for having been party to something so idiotic.

'Been tried? But who . . . who'd be stupid enough . . .?' Jinx didn't have to go on. She only half heard a vague comment from the nursing Sister about 'somebody from the boat'.

Brian Roberts! Of course. It was just the kind of juvenile thing the redheaded fool would get involved in. Jinx knew Brian thought the world of Will Jacobs, and he was young enough and stupid enough to let himself be conned by the old fisherman.

'Tall, skinny, red hair?' She hardly needed the nod from the Sister.

'Mightn't still have red hair. The way Race Morgan got stuck into him, it might very well be white by now,' said Sister Watson. 'I thought for a moment we'd have another patient.'

Jinx sighed, shaking her mop of unruly curls. 'That's all I need,' she muttered. 'Not much wonder Captain Morgan was so angry—and he'll be blaming it all on me.'

'You weren't even here!'

Will might be unrepentant, but he was quick to her defence for all that.

'Brian's part of my crew, even if I didn't hand-pick him. Captain Morgan will blame me; already does.'

'Don't be ridiculous. He's not that type at all.'

The challenge, surprisingly, came not from Will, but from the Sister. Which left Jinx speechless for a moment, unwilling to discuss Race Morgan with a perfect stranger.

She could only stand and stare, meeting soft, melting brown eyes and a smile that suddenly made it all too clear why Will Jacobs so obviously thought Sister Watson was a bit of all right.

'If anything, Race would shoulder the blame himself,'

the nurse continued. 'The young idiot is attached to his
boat, after all.'

'That young idiot is part of *my* scientific crew,' Jinx
insisted. 'Which makes him *my* responsibility and subject
to *my* discipline, as he'll learn to his sorrow when I get
back to the boat.'

'Don't be too tough on the lad,' muttered Will in his
first display of conscience. 'I fed him a pretty good yarn,
and I reckon Race has already disciplined him enough.'

'I'll handle my own crew,' Jinx vowed, though she
knew full well the skipper was the ultimate authority on
any boat. During their previous cruises, she and Will had
shared a good working relationship, one in which
consultation, however noisy and undiplomatic, had
played a real part.

With Race Morgan, she thought as she left the hospital,
things might not be so comfortable. He was a tough man,
much tougher than Will Jacobs even at his best, and far
more used to having his own way.

What bothered her most was the possibility of his
asserting too much authority over her own people, a
situation that by its very existence could undermine her
leadership and disciplinary requirements.

She was long inured to the hassles of being a woman
with authority in a man's world, even the very macho
world of the fishing fleets. And after a few early
difficulties, she'd become sure of her ability to handle
almost any situation.

Young Brian was a handful at the best of times, and she
didn't yet know who the other two members of the
scientific team would be. Compared to the new skipper,
however, none could threaten much in the way of
problems.

Or so she thought until she returned to the *Perfidy* and
met the rest of her team!

CHAPTER TWO

JINX stopped in her tracks, unwilling for a moment to believe her luck. All of it bad—so bad she had an instant's believe that she was, herself, jinxed.

She'd never before seen the tall figure who dominated the crowd on the afterdeck, but there was no mistaking the identity.

Jinx had heard too many tales about Vivian Doherty to be mistaken; the worst part was that everything she'd heard promised nothing but trouble during the month ahead.

If it was true, she thought. Certainly the physical description was spot-on, which made the possibility of the rest being accurate and uncomfortably likely.

Trouble with a capital T, then. Even Race Morgan might find difficulty keeping Vivian Doherty in line.

The skipper was nowhere in evidence when Jinx made her way aboard to find that the much-talked-about Vivian had taken control of both Jinx's own crew and the boat's crew as well.

Tall, perhaps five foot nine, Vivian could only be described as statuesque. Her voluptuous figure was clad in the briefest shorts Jinx had ever seen, and a bikini top that very nearly wasn't. Vivian's waist-length ponytail was undeniably beautiful, except that Jinx had just taken an immediate dislike to auburn hair, she thought.

Even as she approached the deck area where Vivian had the male crew members entranced, Jinx found her mind recalling some of the more vitriolic comments she'd heard about this woman.

Certainly Vivian had created quite a reputation for herself during relatively few years in some nebulous position with the Department of Primary Industry.

'She's the kind who'll trip a bloke and beat him to the floor,' one of Jinx's colleagues had reported after returning exhausted from a conference the redhead had also attended.

Less charitable comments ranged from 'insatiable' through 'nymphomaniac' to 'pure, unadulterated bitch!' All of which spelled trouble on a cruise where everybody was forced into such close quarters that privacy was an impossible luxury, Jinx thought.

She was personally quite broad-minded about other people's morals; what bothered her most about the tales concerning Vivian were the 'bitch' allegations.

Vivian was the type, apparently, who revelled in using her sexuality to pit one man against another. Or, as one especially lurid tale held it, one crew against another. She was reputed to have turned one scientific cruise a year earlier into a total shambles of drunkenness, brawls and wounded feelings.

'Just my luck,' Jinx muttered to herself as she approached the afterdeck, still unnoticed by anyone except the woman at the centre of attention.

And Vivian, of course, would notice her arrival. Vivian would be aware of any female within her range, Jinx thought uncharitably as cool green eyes surveyed her approach.

The eyes narrowed as the crew members recognised the newcomer; clearly Vivian didn't go much on sharing centre stage, either.

'Jinx! But you can't be here—it isn't even raining,' shouted Dick French, the impossibly tall, impossibly thin first mate of the *Perfidy*.

He strode forward to lift Jinx high in the air, kissing her

soundly and with gusto before he dropped her to land with
a thud on the deck.

'And you haven't grown, either,' he jeered. 'I think
you do it deliberately just to keep me from working my
wicked way with you.'

The second crewman known to Jinx only grinned in
welcome. 'Tiny' was probably the most taciturn man
she'd ever known, yet one of the warmest. He was a
mixed-blood, a racial mixture containing Australian
Aborigine, Malay, Chinese and /or Japanese and almost
certainly some South Sea Islander blood as well. He was
built like a Sumo wrestler, had no formal education, and
his idea of a long conversation was three words in a row,
but his knowledge of the sea and its denizens was
encyclopdaedic.

Jinx liked him; he liked her; and for both of them that
was quite sufficient. His presence, she knew, would be a
godsend no matter what else happened.

It was left to Dick to make the introductions of the other
crew, and he started with Vivian, whose eyes remained
agate-hard despite a warm, welcoming smile.

Then there was Glen James, the third of Jinx's boffins.
Glen was short, dark, apparently shy, and about as vocal
as Tiny.

The final boat's crew member was a slightly balding,
weedy little man named George Smith, and he was so
totally nondescript as to hardly exist at all. The type you'd
forget entirely while he was standing talking to you, Jinx
thought, and reproved herself for being so uncharitable.

Besides, he was boat's crew, which made him Race
Morgan's problem if any at all. Jinx had her own crew to
worry about, and with Vivian Doherty involved she'd
have worries enough of her own.

And best, she decided, to at least try to get off to a
pleasant start. Think positively! Vivian, whatever her

faults, at least had fishing experience, and nobody had ever complained about her willingness to work.

Brian was a known quantity, and manageable, Jinx was certain. But Glen James?

'Is this your first trip?' she asked the quiet youth, who flushed slightly at the question, then took his time before answering.

'First with sharks. Fished for mackerel. Blue-fin tuna out of Port Lincoln, spent some time on a prawn trawler.'

'Well, you won't find this much different,' she said with a warm smile. With that sort of experience behind him, at least she could be reasonably expectant that he knew how to work.

'How about you, Vivian? I understand you've a good deal of fishing experience. Any on projects like this?'

'I know about fishing. And fishermen.' There was a note of condescension in the reply, almost a sneer, but still short of a direct challenge to Jinx's authority. She decided to ignore it. For now, at any rate.

Then she was simply forced to ignore it, because Vivian's eyes shifted to focus behind Jinx, and in the process underwent an astonishing transformation. The purity of feeling revealed was so total, so naked, that Jink found herself almost recoiling from the intensity that radiated like heat from the tall redhead's voluptuous figure.

My God! Jinx thought irreverently. In a minute she'll have every man on board snorting and growling and pawing the deck!

A gravelly voice in her ear destroyed that train of thought, and none too soon either, Jinx decided as she turned to face a glowering Captain Race Morgan.

'I'll see you in my cabin if you've a minute, Dr Beaumont,' he said without preamble, and turned away without waiting for a reply.

Brusque but effective, Jinx thought as she trotted in his
wake. Only . . . why? Surely he didn't intend to play
Captain Bligh for the entire cruise; if he did it would
make things totally unbearable, unworkable.

She followed Race Morgan up the steps to his cabin
and inside, fully expecting to be on the receiving end of a
blast about something else she was somehow responsible
for without even knowing it. She would have to clarify the
Brian Roberts situation, if he gave her any chance.

It would be that subject, surely, that Morgan would
want to discuss. He would know she'd have found out by
now, would want to know just how she intended to
implement her own handling of the matter.

I wonder what he expects, she pondered. Keelhauling,
maybe? Walking the plank? He must know I can't cut
Brian's salary, probably couldn't even sack him if I
wanted to.

The need for such harsh discipline had never yet
occurred in Jinx's career. She'd had her share of less
serious problems with staff under her direction, and more
than her share of men whose chauvinism and/or romantic
inclinations needed serious curbing for the sake of the
work at hand. But not anything quite like this.

She waited while Race Morgan seated himself in the
captain's chair, waited again until he roughly gestured for
her to seat herself on the wide bed, there being no other
chair in the cabin. Waited, and became increasingly tense
as he surveyed her in silence, his eyes roving insolently
along the length of her bare legs, then caressing a path up
her body before meeting and holding her own glance.

'Well . . . how is the old man?'

Jinx felt as if somebody had stuck a pin in her. The
brief, growled question was too unexpected in the light of
the hiding she'd been building up for.

'Cranky, noisy, belligerent. And scared stiff, I think,

although he's trying so hard to hide it he's likely to give himself another heart attack just from the strain.'

'That'd be right.' He paused, scowling brow dark over those incredible ice-green eyes. 'I suppose he told you about that young idiot trying to smuggle him in grog?'

Jinx shook her head sadly. 'He sort of mentioned it, although not without some heavy prodding from Sister Watson. Thank God for her! I think if anybody can keep him in line, she will.'

'Don't bet on it.'

And now his expression of concern matched the way Jinx felt. It was somehow gratifying, even if somehow out of character for the role she'd assigned Race Morgan.

It gave her the courage to question his enigmatic comment. 'And what's that supposed to mean?'

He shrugged, the gesture creating a flow of muscle beneath the immaculate T-shirt but not lessening the tautness of his attitude.

'It means she couldn't keep him in line when she was married to him—although to be fair she was younger then. And she's outlived a second husband who was an even worse proposition than Will.'

'I . . . I . . .' Jinx didn't know what to say. One of the few things she'd never discussed with Will Jacobs was marriage, and indeed she had never found herself wondering if he ever had been married. He was such a stereotyped wild, free-spirited bachelor type that she had naturally presumed he'd never attempted to try and settle.

'You can't imagine the old range bull married,' Race Morgan growled, finishing off her thought neatly. 'Neither could he, which is why it's never worked for him.'

He watched the question forming in her eyes, then silently held up two fingers, shook his head in negation, held up three, then four, and finally five fingers before he nodded.

'Bliss Watson was number two, or maybe three,' he said. 'I've never been able to keep track of them all, and frankly wasn't all that interested.'

'Neither was he, from the look of it,' Jinx replied, surprised to find herself angered by the revelation.

'Too interested, more like it. Not that it's any of our business anyway. Waht do you think of your crew for this voyage?'

'I think one of them's going to be starting under a big black thundercloud, for starters,' Jinx replied. 'And if he isn't very, very careful, he's liable to be struck by lightning. If he's lucky.'

'From which I gather you reckon you can handle young Roberts. What about the show pony?'

Jinx couldn't help the explosion of laughter that was provoked by Race Morgan's evocative description. She had a brief but hilarious mental picture that couldn't be resisted no matter how rude it was.

'I can handle her work, assuming she's prepared to do any. Anything . . . else, I suppose, is more in your line,' she finally replied—and went wide-eyed inside at her own cattiness.

Did she only imagine Race Morgan's lip curling in a slight sneer of distaste? And more important, why did that infinitesimal gesture give her such a warm feeling inside?

Jinx met his gaze, and decided she'd imagined it all. She must have.

Race Morgan, for his part, ignored both cattiness and the implied question.

'I gather from Will that you've gone west for all your previous voyages,' he said. 'And that you're a crash-hot cruise leader, a good worker, and you've got a sensible head on your shoulders.'

'I'm really looking forward to seeing something a bit different,' Jinx replied carefully. Inwardly, she was astonished at such strong praise from Will Jacobs, despite knowing his opinion of her before Race Morgan mentioned it.

But it wasn't to be as easy as that.

'Given this sensible head, I reckon you'd better have chapter and verse about young Roberts' indiscretions,' he said then, and the look in his eye told Jinx it wasn't going to be a pleasant recitation.

Five minutes later, she was adamant.

'I'll fire him! Now! Or better yet, let's take him to some deserted island and leave him for the crocodiles,' she raged. 'The idiot! Oh, the stupid, childish fool! Oh, I hope it's true that I'm a jinx,' she snarled finally throught gritted teeth. 'I hope the entire voyage is stormy and that Brian Roberts is seasick the whole time!'

'Thus, with typically feminine logic, inflicting his punishment on everybody else,' Race Morgan replied with a grin. 'So if you are a witch, or whatever it takes to earn a reputation like that, please have a bit of consideration for the rest of us. It'll be bad enough being saddled with the show pony.'

Jinx exploded. She simply couldn't help it.

The outburst of laughter swamped whatever else Race Morgan was about to say, and after an initial scowl, he recognised the pun and laughed with her.

'I'm sorry,' she managed to gasp. 'It's just that I'm a sucker for puns.'

'There are worse sins.'

His voice was still ragged from the laughter, but now Jinx saw in his eyes something of the complex nature of this man. Even while laughing with her, he seemed to remain constantly in a state of assessment, more aware of Jinx herself than of what she was saying.

And he had, she discovered, a disconcerting habit of changing tack without warning. It would have served him well in the days of sail, but for her it presented immediate problems.

'We won't be able to share command the way you did with Will,' he said abruptly, and captured her with his stare, daring her to object.

Jinx returned the gaze, searching her mind for the right words, the exact words to sort this out now, immediately and for the duration. But Race Morgan didn't give her the chance.

'And it's not for the reasons you're thinking,' he said. 'I would normally have no objection at all to such an open arrangement, but under existing circumstances . . .'

He let the words trail off, and in his eyes Jinx saw the abrupt switch of thought that had been triggered by the squeal of laughter from the deck. Then, just as quickly, his eyes focused on her once more.

'I may have to come down on young Miss Doherty very hard indeed at some point on this voyage,' he continued then as if the pause hadn't existed. 'And if it happens to be for something that also involves your work, I don't want any demarcation disputes between you and me to confuse the issues.'

'I think I can understand that,' Jinx said cautiously.

'You'd better.' And there was no compromise in his voice.

Then he continued, his voice gentle again, 'We will, of course, have to consult regularly on all sorts of things, but we won't be doing it as any kind of public forum.' And he grinned, teeth flashing sharklike against the dark mahogany tan. 'So you'd better get used to the feel of that bunk, Dr Beaumont, because you may be spending more time there than you'd think likely.'

They both caught the innuendo, the sudden flash of

intense intimacy that came with it. Race's grin widened,
but Jinx lost all sense of humour.

'I'd say that would be a pretty stupid thing to do,' she
snapped. 'It would only cause all sorts of unnecessary
speculation without accomplishing anything positive at
all.'

'And you don't think your reputation would stand it?'
He was still grinning, but now there was mockery in his
eyes, along with the satisfaction of having reached so
easily through her protective machanisms.

'My reputation isn't relevant to the issue,' she said
coldly. 'The success of my work is! And I can live without
the hassles of being the chief source of rumours that can
do nothing but harm my own authority and my
relationship with my crew.'

Race Morgan didn't reply directly. One dark eyebrow
raised in mocking speculation before he said, 'I have no
intention of interfering in that.'

'And I have no intentionof being hauled in here like a
truant child every time you feel the need for a . . . a
consultation,' Jinx snapped. 'It isn't necessary and I won't
have it.'

'But you haven't got a better suggestion, either,' was
the reply, in a silken, smoky voice that only added to her
irritation.

'My suggestion,' Jinx said haughtily, 'is that you shift
Vivian in here for *consultations*. That would preserve your
own reputation and keep her in line at the same time.'

'Captain's perks?'

'If you choose to call it that, yes.' She spat out her
answer, trying desperately to ignore the cold feeling of
alarm that had begun with her own suggestion.

Logic said it was the best solution to the entire potential
problem of Vivian—for both of them. But even having
spoken it aloud couldn't stop Jinx from wishing she

hadn't even thought it.

Especially when Race Morgan, holding her with his eyes as he did so, gave the suggestion a lengthy, silent consideration. He didn't, however, bother to reveal his final decision.

'What do you say we postpone this consultation until later, since the venue isn't to your liking?' he asked abruptly. 'Since it's our last night ashore for a while, I expect both crews will be out on a rage—except for young Roberts who's under house arrest. We could go and have dinner somewhere and try talking about it like civilised people.'

Civilised? There was nothing about this man to even suggest the word, Jinx thought. He was the very antithesis of civilised. He was a pirate, a barbarian.

'I'd prefer to just leave it, for now,' she told him against the sudden inner desire to take him up on the offer. 'I've been so busy it'll do me good to have a restful night.'

'And how restful do you expect it to be once that lot comes whooping in at some ungodly hour?' He wasn't being especially persuasive, just realistic, she thought, and immediately wondered if he wouldn't really have preferred to spend his last night ashore in other company.

'The later they are, the more rest I'll get,' she replied, then added, 'And if they all stay together there won't be that much disruption when they get back. The problems will come if we have rough going tomorrow.'

He grinned then. 'Which is what the weather man is calling for, in case you hadn't heard. But then that's what you were planning to conjure up, wasn't it?'

'I was actually hoping this trip would mean the end of my reputation along those lines,' Jinx replied with just a hint of a smile in reply. 'I'm getting heartily sick of being thought of as a Jonah. I don't know if Will told you, but we spent nearly half of the last voyage at anchor because it was too rough to travel, let alone fish.'

'Well, maybe this trip will change your luck,' Race shrugged. 'Tomorrow's weather is just passing, and after that it should go well unless we hit some new change up round the Wessels.'

He turned, gesturing towards where he had several charts spread out on the table. 'While you're here, you might as well have a check on the route we'll be taking.'

'I already have,' Jinx told him. A lifetime's fascination with maps had caused her to go out and buy everything available once she'd known she'd been chosen for this particular voyage. She had also done extensive research into the fascinating area she was soon to visit.

The Wessel Islands, a long chain of relatively low islands stretching north-eastward from Arnhem Land, formed the north-eastern tip of the Northern Territory. The Wessels linked the Arafura Sea to the Gulf of Carpentaria. The islands had been named for the *Wessel*, which explored the area in 1637 in company with the *Klem-Amsterdam*. Before that, according to some sources, the group had been known as the Speult Islands, a name provided by the *Arnhem* which had sailed there in 1623. It was an area significant for the fishery of black tip shark, the mainstay of a growing Taiwanese and Australian fishing industry, which was the reason for Jinx's research trip.

Quite without realising it, Jinx found herself leaning over the table as Race Morgan's finger traced their route from Darwin Harbour, and she was so engrossed in the chart that she was only peripherally aware of the strong, blunt fingers, permanently etched by years of working with nets and lines.

They would sail north at first, around the Vernons, through Van Diemen Gulf and out through Dundas Strait

into the Arafura Sea. Then the run would be to the east,
straight across the top of Australia until they reached the
Wessels. They would—if the tides and weather were
right—sail the *Perfidy* through Gugari Rip, a narrow,
potentially dangerous channel between Guluwuru Island
and Raragala Island, Race said.

'But we only do it if everything's right. Going against
the tide in that narrow little gash between the cliffs is a
tricky business for a vessel like this one.'

He grinned, eyes revealing that risk-taking was almost
as natural to Race Morgan as eating or sleeping. 'Of
course the prawn trawlers shoot through there under
almost any conditions, but they're all mad anyway.'

If the conditions were wrong to take the 'hole-in-the-
wall' route through Gugari Rip, he said, they'd either go
round past Cape Wessel or swing close in to get through
the Cunninghams, slide through the English Company's
Islands, round Cape Wilberforce and into Melville Bay
and the Gove Peninsula.

'I've got extra bait arranged at Gove, although of
course we'll take plenty from here as well,' he said. 'I
don't know how much long-lining we'll be doing.'

Jinx hardly heard him, she was so engrossed in the
magic of new but already familiar names on the charts.
Names from history and prehistory, linking the
adventures of the traditional owners, the Aborigines, with
those of the visiting Dutch, Portuguese, Malaysian and
English seamen.

Many of the islands had been named from Matthew
Flinders' expedition of 1803, and of these, she best liked
the story of the English Company's Islands. Flinders had
named almost all of them individually for gentlemen of
the East India Directory because of support given his
expeditions by the Company. But while he was anchored
during February in a roadstead south of the English

Company's group, he was visited by several Malay captains on vessels in search of bêche-de-mer, the sea cucumber considered a delicacy by the Chinese.

One of these captains, named Pobasso or Pobassoo, claimed to have been the first of his people to come to Arnhem Land nearly thirty years earlier, so Flinders had obligingly named one of the English Company's islands for him. Jinx had chuckled upon turning up that piece of information, wondering how the esteemed gentlemen of the East India Company would have liked the gesture.

She returned to the present to catch the tail end of Race Morgan's comments, just enough to realise he was telling her that Marchinbar Island, which terminated in Cape Wessel, was called Ermibiga in the local Aboriginal dialect. She waited, hoping he would explain the meaning, but any explanation was forestalled by the unexpected arrival of a tall, slender young blonde. The woman strode into the cabin without knocking, her voice already sighing Race's name in a breathless cry of welcome when she saw Jinx and stopped as if she'd run into an invisible wall.

'I . . . I'm so sorry, Race darling,' she said after a moment's tense pause. 'I just never thought you might have somebody with you.'

'Not just somebody, Melissa. This is Dr Beaumont, who's in charge of the scientific crew on our cruise,' said Race, then went on to introduce Jinx to Melissa Stewart.

There was no more than the introduction. Nothing to explain who the blonde was, or where she fitted into the dark captain's life. Jinx made her excuses and left as soon as possible, annoyed that she wondered about that.

Race Morgan emerged from the cabin not long afterwards, the blonde hanging on to him with possessive skill, and paused on the foredeck only long enough to announce final shore leave for everyone except Brian Roberts.

'No getting in trouble, and I'd suggest you keep the drinking down to something reasonable, because we sail at dawn no matter what the weather,' he said.

And then, surprisingly, he glanced down at Jinx and added another rider.

'Since Dr Beaumont plans to make an early night of it, make damned sure you come aboard quietly when you do,' he remarked with a glowering expression that left no room for argument. It was aimed, Jinx noted, mostly at Vivian and Dick French, who seemed to have paired off together on one corner of the deck.

If Vivian noticed, Jinx couldn't detect any sign. The statuesque redhead was so busy staring daggers at Melissa Stewart that Jinx doubted if a single word had penetrated.

They all watched as Race Morgan strode ashore, the blonde hanging like a limpet from his arm, then everyone but Brian gave a whoop of delight and hurried to the fo'c'sle to change for their own night on the town.

Jinx waited until they'd finished, more than content to hover at the rail and watch the sun sinking into the still, reflective waters of Darwin Harbour. Sundown brought hardly a change to the warmth in the air, and she was comfortable in just her shorts and T-shirt, but her mind wasn't all that comfortable.

Visions of Race Morgan kept creeping up to leap full-blown into her thoughts, and they weren't conducive to a calm evening of reflectiveness.

Brian Roberts didn't help either. He joined Jinx after the others had left, and his first remark was sufficient to warn her that Vivian wasn't the only potential threat to the peacefulness of the coming voyage.

'Morgan's got his nerve, rousting on me for the other night,' Brian began without preamble. 'That Melissa he's chasing around with is young enough to be his daughter.'

'Maybe she is,' Jinx suggested, half joking and half

wishing she could find an easy way to change the subject.

'Not hardly! She's the daughter of one of the top Territory politicians,' Brian replied scornfully. 'One that I hear Morgan has considerable dealings with, although he seems to have as many with his daughter. Half his luck!'

'You'll need more than half his luck if you don't get your act together for the rest of this voyage,' said Jinx. 'What you got involved in the other day was childish and it was stupid—and we both know that. Any more of it and you'll have *me* to contend with, after which you might prefer the skipper any day.'

She caught his glowering, juvenile expression, and silently cursed herself for not expecting this. Brian had shown tendencies on the last voyage to be a childish fool, but she'd made no mention of that in her reports, preferring to give him the benefit of the doubt. Now she'd paid the price.

'I mean it, Brian,' she insisted. 'You do *one* more thing to screw up the scientific team's reputation on this voyage and I'll see you regret it.'

She got a grudging acquiescence and decided, for the moment, to let the matter drop there.

'All right, let's leave it for now,' she said. 'I've promised myself an early night, so I think I'll turn in now and see if I can sleep through the return of the ravening hordes.'

It was a good plan, but it didn't work very well. After showering, she tucked herself into her bunk and truly tried to sleep, but her mind was too contrary to allow it. She found herself thinking of Race Morgan and of the women who were so obviously attracted to him.

Her hatred of Vivian's auburn mane was understandable enough, considering her own rather nondescript tangle of blondish curls, cut passably short,

at least enough to be convenient, thick enough to be
manageable, but still not very imposing. One star-struck
boyfriend had described it as being the colour of good,
leatherwood bush honey, but when compared to the sleek
blonde tresses of Melissa Stewart it didn't really rate.

Nor, she decided, did much else about her. She was
pretty enough, but totally lacked the Junoesque presence
of Vivian or the studied sophistication of Melissa.

Grey-blue eyes, thick dark eyebrows, a distinctly pug
nose she'd never much liked. Round face, good teeth and
a smile that had been described as her very best feature.

Good legs, though, she decided. And a good figure
when not being compared to something like Vivian's
undeniably striking presence.

She decided she could hate tall women very easily.

And with that decision came the obvious question. Was
Race Morgan the catalyst for this sudden bout of self-
analysis?

He was certainly a striking figure, a startlingly
attractive if not truly handsome man, and a man whose
magnetic presence couldn't be ignored. But she'd only
just met him! Jinx thought for an instant, then smiled in
the dark safety of the bunk. Just met him . . . and been
kissed by him . . . and liked it.

She drifted into sleep, the warm scent of the tropical
night a balm to her troubled thoughts, and woke only
briefly at the arrival of the crew well past midnight. When
she woke again, it was only an hour later, and there was
no apparent reason. Until she heard the soft hum of voices
from the deck above and recognised the rumbling tones of
the skipper's voice, mingled with a softer, female voice
that could only be Melissa's. And while she didn't mean
to eavesdrop, it was impossible not to. The voices had
startling clarity.

'Do you really have to be gone for a whole month,

darling?'

Jinx found herself hating the exquisite blonde just for the smarmy tone in that voice, the studied little-girl quality that was being used for all it was worth.

Was Race Morgan unaware of it? she wondered, then decided he couldn't possibly be. Whether his womanising reputation was deserved or not, he certainly was no novice when it came to the opposite sex.

'Could be longer. Depends on the weather, how the scientific work goes.'

His voice showed no sign of playing to the plaintive qualities of the blonde. It was, like the rest him, blunt and direct.

'But why do *you* have to go as skipper? Surely you could send somebody else. Oh, Race, I'm just going to miss you *so* much. You know I get so lonely when you're gone.'

The silence that followed needed no words, and Jinx found herself angrily wishing Race Morgan would conduct his love affairs in the privacy of his own cabin.

None of the others in the fo'c'sle would hear; they were dead to the world, and deservedly so. For an instant she wished she'd gone off carousing with them; the hangover would have been easier to take than this enforced sharing of an intimacy she found profoundly distasteful.

Then that hated little-girl voice started up again, grating on Jinx's eardrums as much as it grated on her mind.

'Race, why don't we go up to your cabin? It would be so much more . . . comfortable.'

'Because it's late and it's time you were home in your own little bed. I'm going to have a long, rough day tomorrow as it is.'

'Oh, Race!'

'Oh, nothing. You've been a doll to give me a lift back; now don't push your luck.'

Jinx lay still in her bunk, fascinated now. Was this the legendary Race Morgan, lover? Refusing what surely must be considered very tempting bait indeed?

'You're not being very nice to me.'

'I'm being as nice as I intend to be,' came the gruff reply. 'Now go home before I stop being nice and decide to give you the licking your father ought to.'

'I'd tell him if you did.' And Jinx could sense the threat in that comment, which said far more than just the words. Had Race caught it as well?

'For which he'd thank me,' was the skipper's reply, followed—astonishingly—by the undeniable sound of a smack.

Jinx found herself tensing, waiting for the squeal that must follow. Unless of course the sound was from Race Morgan's face being slapped.

'That hurt!'

'Not as much as the next one will. Now off you go and do your sulking in your own time. Mine belongs to the ship for the next month.'

'But you'll be seeing me as soon as you get back?' Again the plaintive tones, but Race seemed hardly impressed.

'We'll see. I'll talk to your father when I seem him at Gove, and ask if you've been behaving or not.'

There was a tinkle of girl-child laughter.

'You know I'm always good, except maybe with you.'

Lies, thought Jinx. This one is a born liar, a born seductress.

'Little bitch,' she whispered into the security of her pillow, then half sat up, wide-eyed, at the recognition of her own vehemence.

Outside, the noises told her of Melissa's still-complaining departure, but even the eventual silence that followed didn't allow a return to sleep.

Jinx waited, restless, for perhaps fifteen minutes, then slipped on her T-shirt and shorts and quietly tiptoed up the companionway to the main deck. Coffee, she thought as she headed for the galley, eyes adjusted to the tropic darkness so that she easily found her way.

Beneath her, the boat rocked gently on the incoming tide, and she felt herself relaxing, eager now to be starting this voyage, to be going somewhere new, somewhere totally different.

She fired up the gas stove, hunted out the instant coffee while the kettle boiled, and had just poured her drink when some inner sense made her aware that she wasn't alone.

'You can make me a cup too, if you wouldn't mind,' said Race Morgan's rumbling voice as she turned to face him.

To her credit, Jinx had excellent nerves and better reflexes. She neither registered alarm nor dropped the coffee cup she was holding.

'I'd have thought you'd be asleep long ago,' she said, using the making of his cup to keep from looking at him as she lied.

'I've never been able to sleep well just before a voyage,' he replied with unexpected candour. 'I've no idea where the tenseness comes from, but it doesn't seem to be curable, so I've learned to live with it.'

And I can imagine some of the cures you've attempted, thought Jinx with uncharacteristic cattiness, her mind picturing Melissa Stewart in a role the blonde child-woman could handle very competently indeed.

'Do you go to sea often? Yourself, I mean,' she asked cursing herself for her clumsiness. 'I would have thought that as owner of the fleet you'd be ashore a lot, organising, that sort of thing.'

'I'm ashore far more than I like,' he replied, raising

those incredible ice-green eyes to capture her gaze and hold her, almost mesmerising her with the intensity of his glance. 'And what's your excuse for being up at this ungodly hour? Don't tell me you got such an early night that you're slept out?'

'Something like that,' she admitted. 'I just woke a minute ago and knew I wouldn't get back to sleep again, so I'm here.'

Lies, lies and damned lies, she thought, but knew she must cover any possibility that he might suspect she'd overheard his farewell performance with Melissa.

And was that what had just occurred to him? He didn't reply for a moment, but sat idly revolving his coffee-cup betwen tanned, muscular hands, and mesmerising her with his eyes, sensitising her to his look.

Jinx could almost imagine those strong fingers touching her body, not the cup, could almost imagine the combination of strength and gentleness, the experienced skills inherent there. For a moment she seemed to float, to hover outside herself. And she realised her breath was coming in short gasps through lips that were parted invitingly, that her own eyes were softened with desire.

And worse yet, she realised that Race Morgan saw her in exactly the same way, that he had stopped fiddling with the cup, that something was passing between them, transmitted through their eyes.

Jinx shook her head, raised one hand to paw through her tousled curls. This was dangerous, she decided, and would have run from the room except that to reach the only exit meant passing within reach of him.

Strangely, Race did nothing at all. He just sat there, his attention once again diverted to the cup in his hands, or to whatever his gaze had now become attracted. Not fortunately, Jinx herself, she decided.

'You really ought to do something about that,' he

drawled slowly, and when she looked up at him his eyes pounced, locking her in yet again.

'About what?' Stupid question, and yet . . . whatever did he mean?

'About your astonishing habit of sending out conflicting sexual signals at one and the same time,' he replied, and grinned that wicked devil's grin when Jinx recoiled, startled by his perception.

'I . . . don't know what you mean,' she said.

'Obviously.' And now his voice was dry, rumbling like distant thunder just to enunciate that one word. 'That's why I brought it up, because it's something you damned well shouldn't do *without* being aware of it. You'll get yourself in trouble that way some day.'

I'm in trouble now, thought Jinx, but didn't say it.

'I wasn't aware that I was sending out any sort of signals at all. I certainly didn't intend to,' she said. 'Are you sure you're not imagining things?'

'Nope.'

The pause was hypnotic. And when she finally spoke, it was with the realisation of her earlier vision. She had been sending out signals all right, and she'd been doing so because he had been demanding them, had been practically orchestrating them.

'I think you're mad,' she told him as scathingly as she could manage, and leaned back in her chair, half expecting him now to try and push the issue further, perhaps physically.

But he didn't. He just sat and looked at her, his eyes roving insolently from her hair to her breasts and back again, assessing, interpreting, imprinting.

'You needn't be so paranoid about it,' he said. 'I just thought it was something you should be aware of if you weren't already, that's all.'

'Why?'

'Because you don't impress me as the type who'd get pleasure out of deliberately misleading people.'

And with that, he rose to his feet, stretching until his muscular body seemed to fill the tiny galley, until all Jinx could be aware of was the power of that body, the taut, concentrated masculinity of it.

He glanced at his wristwatch, twisted his mobile, generous mouth into a moue of distaste, and turned towards the door.

'There's time for another hour's kip, I suppose,' he said over one broad shoulder. 'I'm going to try for it and I suggest you do too. We're going to be in for some rugged going once we're past Cape Don.'

'Just so you don't say it's my fault,' Jinx retorted to his departing back, thinking immediately about a past voyage, where she'd spent hours on her back beneath the mess table, so seasick she wouldn't have dared move even if she'd been able to.

'I'll reserve judgement,' said Race over his shoulder. 'Who knows? Maybe you send scrambled signals to the weather man too.'

'I wish you'd get off that subject!' she cried, only just restraining herself from throwing something at that arrogant back. 'I'm not sending any kind of signals, and if I were, they wouldn't be sent to you, Mr Morgan!'

She was on her feet, prepared to leave the galley once he provided room to move, but she wasn't prepared for the speed with which he turned in his tracks, bringing them face to face in the narrow intimacy of the passageway.

Their eyes met, locked. He didn't touch her, but didn't need to. It was as if invisible hands were on her neck, lightly stroking from the lobes of her ears to the soft hollows above her collarbones.

Again Jinx could feel her breathing quicken, her mouth

soften as if in preparation for a kiss. Her vision blurred until all she could see were the deep wells of his eyes.

'*Captain* Morgan,' he whispered in a voice that rumbled softly. 'Remember it, or the only signals being flown will be distress signals. From you. Unmistakable, not confused, not scrambled.'

Jinx couldn't reply. His lips were only inches away, and although he hadn't touched her, it was as if he were constantly touching her.

Suddenly she became aware of his desire, knew it by the change in his eyes, the slight shift in his stance. And knew he meant her to become aware of it.

She was powerless beneath his gaze, realised that she was being drawn to his lips as if by some magnetic force, by the magnetic force of a personality stronger than any she'd ever encountered.

When their lips met, it wasn't a matter of Race kissing her. *She* kissed him. *She* initiated the move, *she* lifted her lips to meet his, *she* invoked the taste of him, the touch of him.

But *he* ended the kiss, and worse, he did it with a single, brutal, backward step. Jinx was caught almost off balance and nearly stumbled fair into his arms.

She recovered to find him grinning, the grin a mockery of the feelings inside her.

'Better,' he said. 'Much better.'

Then he turned and was gone before the first tear began its tormented path down her cheek.

CHAPTER THREE

THEY sailed with the dawn, chugging northwards out of Darwin Harbour and then into the face of a sun tormented by scudding cloud.

Jinx fretted mildly throughout the first day, so miserable in her mind that the encroaching symptoms of seasickness could almost be ignored.

Others of the combined crew weren't so lucky. The grog they'd drunk the night before now produced anything but a convivial mood, with the boat pitching as it tackled the bow seas.

Only Race Morgan—*Captain* Morgan, she remembered to think—seemed impervious to the effects of the heavy weather upon the boat and its crew. He stood in the wheelhouse, muscular hands almost toying with the wheel, body relaxed to the sea's movement.

Perhaps the only consolation was that Brian Roberts was just as sick as Jinx might have predicted—fitting punishment, she thought, for his abominable behaviour ashore.

He wasn't sick enough, unfortunately, to stop him doing everything in his weakened power to blame the weather and its effects on her. Not that anybody seemed to be listening; they were all too much affected by the pitching motion of the boat to care what anybody thought.

The enclosed fo'c'sle was abandoned. None of them could handle being in such a confined space under such foul conditions. Far better to be on deck, where at least they could see the horizon, try to orientate their abused bodies to the ship's erratic motion.

The torture continued until nearly evening, when the south-easterly trade winds abated somewhat, and the most hardy of the crew could muster sufficient energy to at least think about preparing a meal.

It wasn't much; the blandness of poached eggs on toast was considered about all anybody could stand, and there were several who turned up noses and stomachs even at that.

Jinx ate, as did Race Morgan, but it was an effort.

One unexpected advantage, however, was finding that, once they'd put to sea, Race seemed to lose a lot of his arrogance, a lot of the distance factor that had tended to set him aside from everyone else in Jinx's mind.

Although it was indefinably clear from the beginning that he was the skipper, that he was ultimately in charge, he never seemed to go out of his way to make a point of it. Not, she decided, that he really needed to. The man just seemed to wear his authority like a nearly-invisible mantle. He was the type of person literally born to walk in paths of authority; a natural leader.

Just how much so became apparent almost immediately the first scientific crew member proved susceptible to *mal de mer*, or seasickness. Race Morgan didn't laugh, nor did he rage at the inconvenience that was certain to follow as the other crew members succumbed. While he showed no personal susceptibility, it was clear that he realised seasickness was something they'd all have to live with until it was over, and with eight of them crowded into the small fishing craft, adaptability was the only solution. And adaptability would have to include a decent sense of humour.

'Are you going to prove immune to the bad weather you're being accused of having provided?' he asked Jinx as they forced down the makeshift meal.

'I'm not sure,' she replied honestly, and leaned over to peer at the semi-conscious figure of Brian Roberts, who lay flat on his back, moaning in despair and staring fixedly upward at the underside of the mess table where they sat.

'That's where I was, next-to-last voyage,' she said. 'I believe I can still draw you a chart of every knothole and detail of that table from underneath.'

Both of them sat with legs tucked under to avoid kicking poor Brian, who was, for the moment, oblivious to their conversation.

Dick French had recovered sufficiently to stand watch and give the skipper a break, while Tiny hung over the stern rail, showing some signs of recovery.

But the remainder of the scientific crew would be of little use until morning, Jinx had decided. The lovely Vivian had finally made it to her bunk, and if Brian and Glen James could do the same—given no return of the bad winds—tomorrow might seem a new day indeed.

'I hope you're not feeling guilty about this,' Race said with a suggestion of a grin. Not a proper smile, but a quirk of his lips that made it difficult for Jinx to tell if he was being sympathetic or just readying her for some further accusation.

'You don't think I should?' Her own smile was rueful. 'If I really am a jinx, I've done a good job this time. Tiny . . . seasick? If I hadn't seen it, I wouldn't have believed it for a minute.'

'Nothing to do with anything being your fault. It was I who decided to sail when we did. I knew what was coming weather-wsie; did you?'

'Only that you said it might be tricky,' she admitted. 'But you may have trouble convincing Tiny of that. He's very superstitious, you know.'

Race's green eyes flashed with laughter.

'Not about you,' he assured her. 'He's sailed with you before; if he thought you were really a jinx he wouldn't have done it again. And he isn't seasick because of you, either; he's sick because he got drunk last night, just like everybody else.'

'Except you and me. And . . . Brian didn't.'

'Young Roberts is seasick because he expected to be seasick; it's as simple as that,' Race replied. 'And because I set up a situation in which everybody should have been.'

Jinx could only stare as the realisation hit her.

'Deliberately?' The single word emerged as a whisper, needed no reply. Of course he'd done it deliberately. Worse, he'd done so knowing very well she'd catch the flak for it. But why?

His shrug was infuriating, his reply worse.

'It'll make it easier for them to stand up to any normal rough weather,' he said. 'And easier for them to work together, in the long run. There's nothing like a little shared misery to bring a crew together.'

Jinx didn't know what to reply to that. The truth of his remark was self-evident, but to be so deliberate about it . . . *Sadist* came easily to mind.

'I'm not, you know!'

She lifted her eyes to meet a lazy grin, to see ice-coloured eyes with no chill in them. Knowing eyes.

She refused to be drawn. 'Not a sadist? No, you probably aren't. But it doesn't make you any nicer.'

Then she retreated from his stare, retreated from the way he seemed to look into her eyes and reach through them to discover her most intimate feelings, most secret thoughts.

'I suppose I've disappointed you, then, by not getting seasick like everybody else,' she found herself saying—and wondering later whatever would have prompted such an inane remark.

'Surprised, not disappointed,' he replied with a grin. 'But it was probably a good thing. They'll remember that, and it might make your job as leader a bit easier.'

There was something in the way he said it, some nuance of voice that put Jinx's nerves on edge. Or else it was the way he looked at her, into her, through her.

'I've never needed a façade of invincibility to help me run a team before,' she said. 'I'm sufficiently competent to do my job without resorting to that.'

'Oh, yes, you're very competent, I'm sure,' he responded. 'And do you run your life the same way? Always cool, calm and collected?'

'Yes. Why not?'

'Why not indeed?'

His answer was evasive. He knew it was, and the devil's laughter lurked behind his eyes.

Damn the man, she thought. It seemed he had decided his purpose in life was to stir her up, to destroy whatever shreds of complacency might remain in her existence.

Her introspection into that subject was improved not at all by Morgan's departure. He moved so silently, with such animal grace, that the impression of the semi-barbarian was always with him.

She watched his departing back, the muscles so disturbingly revealed by the accepted boat costume of shorts and T-shirt, and wondered if he deliberately made a game out of stirring people, then sitting back to watch the results.

Very likely, she decided. He wouldn't have parlayed his meagre beginnings into a legendary empire without learning, or at least developing, the astuteness into human nature that any natural leader must possess.

Then she glanced down to the moaning figure of Brian Roberts on the floor beneath the mess table, and shook her head sadly. Had Brian overheard their conversation, presuming he could understand it?

She got his answer a few minutes later when Brian groaned louder than usual, and creakily began manoeuvring his lanky frame into an upright position.

'Sadist? He's a proper bastard,' were his first words. So obviously he'd both overheard and understood. 'Of all the bloody nerve! I tell you, Jinx, that man's dangerous. Imagine putting us all through this just for the sake of crew morale!'

Whereupon he tottered off to his bunk in the fo'c'sle, leaving Jinx to ponder that same question over a cup of coffee that had grown cold without her even noticing.

Despite Morgan's blunt admission, she retained a degree of uncertainty about his intentions, and when Dick French wandered in off watch, still showing the signs of the hard day behind him, she couldn't resist the chance to pick his brains on the subject.

'It wouldn't bloody well surprise me,' was the mate's reaction, uttered wearily but entirely without rancour. 'The skipper's a hard one; no question about that. And it would be one way he'd choose to sort out both crews in one easy lesson.'

Jinx nodded, but still wasn't convinced.

'I sort of thought maybe he was just trying to justify my reputation,' she queried. 'Or confirm it for ever, more likely.'

Dick laughed. 'For what, though? No profit in that, and I can tell you that Race Morgan doesn't often do anything without some vision of profit. That's why he's so damned successful.'

'You sound as if you rather like him.'

'I admire him, I suppose. He's gone a long way and he's worked and fought for every inch of the way. But he's a different bloke to sail under from old Will, that's for sure and certain.'

'He reminds me of a pirate.' Jinx made the remark as much to herself as to Dick, so she was slightly surprised when he burst into gales of laughter at the charge.

'He's been accused of it, never fear,' the mate said with a final chuckle. 'And accused of just about every other dirty trick you can think of, as well. Not surprising, I suppose, considering what he's done with his life.'

'And you, for one, don't believe a word of it, I suppose,' Jinx prompted. 'Why not?'

'Because most of it isn't true, of course. He's a hard man, no worries, but he's a fair one. Ask old Will about that, sometimes. Or a score of others I could name.'

He shook his head wearily, staring dreamily down into his coffee cup, then continued, 'No, Race Morgan's as good a man as you'd find, in my book.'

'Even if he deliberately sailed into rough weather so everybody'd get seasick?'

She asked the question almost without thinking, then found herself awaiting his reply with bated breath.

'Why not? We all deserved it for playing up the night before a trip,' the mate replied lightly. 'Besides, a little seasickness never hurt anybody. Good for the system, I reckon, especially after a night on the grog. Now when it comes time for the hard work, we'll all be fit and ready for it, as we should be.'

He was right, and the proof of that came the very next day, when Race met Jinx on deck with the rising sun and pointed to a smudge of land on the southern horizon.

'The Goulburn Islands,' he said. 'Which means this ought to be a good place to shoot the net, see if everybody knows about the work that's ahead.'

'Don't you think it might be nice to have breakfast first?' she found herself replying, only just barely awake and certain nobody else in the fo'c'sle had so much as stirred yet.

He looked hard at her for an instant, then laughed, his teeth gleaming in the early sunlight. Under his T-shirt, muscles flexed like steel cables as he stretched, then relaxed into animal-like ease.

'Don't tell me you're a morning grouch,' he said half seriously. 'I don't think I could live with that.'

'I can't imagine you having to,' Jinx replied peevishly, annoyed at his snap judgement. She was very definitely not a morning grouch. Mornings were the best time of the day for her. 'I was only wondering if you expected me to rouse everybody to start fishing this very minute, or . . . or what?'

'*What* sounds like an even better idea, although it's a bit early in the morning for it,' he said enigmatically. But his eyes, roving across her scantily clad body, left no question about his meaning.

Jinx glared in reply, suddenly all too conscious of her bikini top and shorts, hastily tied sarong.

'And not on an empty stomach, either,' she snapped in a hasty reply, then turned away and did her best to walk briskly away as if his remark didn't matter in the slightest. Not the easiest task; the swaying deck forced an equivalent sway into her stride, and she couldn't help feeling that her attempted confidence would only come out looking like a sexual come-on.

Which is the last thing I need, much less intend, she thought as she ducked into the entrance to the galley and began searching out the makings for her morning coffee.

Damn the man! And it was no consolation to find that his physical attraction hadn't been diminished one iota by the early hour. Much of his innuendo had infuriated her—just as she was certain it was intended to do—there was no deying the instant attraction, either.

The whole situation made her furious, and she was busily banging her way through the galley in search of the instant coffee when Dick French sauntered in.

'Cuppa for me too?' he asked without so much as offering a good morning first. It was the final straw.

'You can damn well get your own,' snapped Jinx, and stalked out, ignoring his expression of surprise.

Race, thank heavens, had returned to his wheelhouse before she emerged on deck. Jinx wandered to the stern of the ship and stood watching the slow turbulence of the sea beneath them, breathing slowly and deeply as she sought to regain her composure.

Five minutes passed, then ten. She turned and marched back to the galley.

'I'm sorry, Dick,' she apologised as she entered. 'I don't know why I was so bitchy.'

'Didn't even notice,' Dick replied. 'Come and have a cuppa; it'll settle your nerves and get you ready for the day.'

'We're going to stop and fish; I suppose you already know that?'

'Good place for it. Should be plenty of shark about here,' he said simply. 'One or two shots ought to take the kinks out of everybody, finish off any hangovers that might be left.'

'Surely there couldn't be any?' laughed Jinx. She had never had a hangover in her life, and although she had been able to sympathise with the crew yesterday, it was far from the sympathy of a fellow sufferer.

'Not much, that's for sure,' he agreed laughingly. 'But nobody'll be at their best for another day or two, you can bet on that.'

The truth of that comment was evident as the remainder of the crew straggled from the fo'c'sle like a weary band of repentant sinners.

Breakfast was a haphazard affair, with nobody very interested in either cooking or eating, and conversation centred on the improvement in the weather. But once Race had gathered everyone on deck, Jinx noticed a general improvement in posture, as if nobody wished to be singled out as a malingerer or continued hangover victim.

'You all know, I'm sure, that we'd normally do our net fishing at night,' Race began. 'But I think a couple of shots now will put everybody into the routine and give me a chance to see how the scientific end of this programme goes.'

His glance caught Jinx's eye, and she wondered if her own expression revealed her surprise. She simply hadn't thought of it, but of course Race Morgan wouldn't have seen the work her own crew did on such a voyage.

'We'll run through it right from the beginning, if you don't mind,' he continued, still holding Jinx with his eyes. 'And then we'll motor eastward and give the long-lines a trial in the process. The weather should be good enough to get us to the Wessels within another couple of days.'

Jinx was pleased to find there was little discussion or need for it, once the five-hundred metre length of fifteen-centimetre mesh had been carefully released from the huge net drum on the stern. The boat's crew, of course, knew exactly what had to be done, and her own group needed only a brief discussion to be equally organised.

Once the net had been 'shot', and the rope at the end attached to the bow roller of the boat, the crew under Race's direction began hauling it in. It was up to Jinx and her group to disengage sharks from the net, measure and tag and inspect them, then return the hunters of the sea to their salty environment.

This was the part of the work she liked best. Stripped to her bikini, she had donned a heavy rubber apron, and stout sea-boots to give her some protection from the sandpapery skin of the sharks.

The net moved slowly along the deck, empty at first, but finally producing the first shark of the voyage, to cheers from both crews. It was a one-metre black-tip, pretty much as expected since this was the most common species in the region and the species upon which the Australian and Taiwanese shark fishery depended most heavily.

Equally predictable was her own reaction. She was so keyed up, so vitally alert, alive, that it seemed to her that her entire world was just a little bit brighter, a little bit more vivid.

Carefully she reached out to grasp the writhing, thrashing predator, using both hands to secure a safe grip that prevented the shark from opening its mouth. Then she moved backwards, her aim to ease the shark free of the mesh so that it could be heaved up on to the hatch cover where the measuring and tagging equipment was set out in readiness.

'Got him!' Another pair of hands joined the fray, and seconds later the shark was being stretched along the measuring board between Jinx and Vivian, while Brian readied the tagging gun.

And so it went throughout the morning, the crew swiftly falling into a work pattern that promised both safety and efficiency for the voyage.

Jinx was at first surprised that it was Vivian who had stepped in to help her with the shark handling, then she realised no specific instruction had been established about that part of the work.

It was no surprise that Glen James was happiest at first to play record-keeper; his lack of shark experience made it logical for the young man to work into the job gradually.

And somehow it was no surprise when, after the second shot was completed, Race called a halt to the proceedings and nodded his own acceptance of her crew's efficiency.

'Smooth . . . very smooth indeed,' he commented as the final clean-up work was completed. Jinx could only agree silently, thankful that his testing exercise had gone so incredibly smoothly. Under more normal circumstances, she knew, there would have been a host of foul-ups and problems, but this crew—it had to be admitted—worked as smoothly as anyone could possibly ask for.

As they chugged eastward through the afternoon, the long-lines with their three hundred hooks were set and retrieved in a monotonous and fruitless pattern that produced only one small shark.

'We'll do better tonight with the nets,' said Race as Jinx glowered at the incoming string of empty hooks, disappointed despite her knowledge that night-time net fishing was always far more productive.

She didn't reply, certain he was only trying to put her at ease, and somehow resentful that he should think she needed such a gesture. It was . . . almost patronising, she thought, especially in view of the good morning's run.

Brian and Glen were down at the stern doing water salinity and temperature checks, while Vivian was perched where she too could observe the slowly returning empty long-line.

Jinx couldn't help but admire the statuesque redhead, despite still being unsure if she could like her or not. Vivian's quiet competence during the morning's fishing seemed to Jinx to be the lull before the storm, or was she just imagining things? Certainly she couldn't fault the work she'd shared.

A sideways glance revealed that Race, also, was admiring the scarcely-concealed figure of the redhead, and he certainly made no secret of his appreciation, Jinx thought.

Then she silently cried out in chastisement at such catty thoughts. What business was it of hers? And worse, to be totally honest, what sort of man would he be if he didn't admire such a splendid example of her sex?

Except, she thought, that it makes me feel all sort of short and dumpy and colourless . . . a real ugly duckling.

While Vivian had deliberately—Jinx was sure!—chosen to work in the briefest of bikinis, she herself was wearing a T-shirt over her own bikini, and a short sarong tightly wrapped below that. Now that Vivian had taken over the infrequent task of wrestling sharks from the hooks to the tagging table, Jinx had no need to swelter in the heavy rubber apron and seaboots, though to be honest she had no justification for the relative modesty of her attire, either. It was just that she found the blatant comparison difficult to cope with, especially on those few occasions she'd glanced up to find Race's speculative eyes not on Vivian, but on Jinx herself.

Not that she could reasonably blame *him* for the way she felt! It was purely a matter of her own choice, of the turmoil of feelings that churned up her insides almost any time he looked at her.

And I do blame him, she thought angrily, admitting to herself that Race Morgan was quite the most disturbing man she'd ever come across. Without doing or saying a single thing, without providing any justifiable evidence of his influence, he had her thinking like a lovesick schoolgirl, or worse.

Worse, because she couldn't seem to stop it, couldn't seem to turn off her mind, to concentrate on her work, on the pleasure of the cruise, the joy of seeing new things, new places. Race Morgan loomed like some primitive spectre at the edge of her consciousness, not exactly intruding, just . . . there.

Even at this moment, with his attention apparently

focused upon the charms of the delectable Vivian Doherty, there was some aspect of the man that registered a subtle awareness of Jinx herself, of her presence, her thoughts.

'Is she going to work out?'

Jinx flinched at the unexpected question.

'On the basis of today's effort, I should certainly think so,' she replied. 'She knows the work, and nobody could ever accuse her of shirking.'

He shrugged, eyes still roving across the redhead's figure in what could only be described as a visual caress. Jinx found herself gritting her teeth, then as quickly relaxed, nearly having to stifle a giggle at the sheer ridiculousness of her unwarranted, illogical jealousy.

'You don't reckon she's taking a bit of a risk, working without protective gear?' Race commented. 'If she isn't careful, she'll lose some skin—or worse. Those little horrors have hides like sandpaper.'

Jinx knew that, having learned it herself the hard way. But she'd also learned the astonishing resilience of human skin, having taken more than her share of cuts and scrapes and abrasions during earlier cruises. Vivian, she thought, ought to know better than to work with no protection at all, but the type of injury risked from that alone was minor enough.

'It's *her* skin,' she replied, voice calm despite a tiny resentfulness at Race's concern.

His slow grin didn't help.

'Sure is,' he drawled softly, using his voice to stretch out the obvious appreciation already evident in his ice-green eyes. 'Pity to see it messed up, I'd reckon.'

Jinx stifled a bitchy reply. He would know as well as she did that minor scrapes and abrasions were unavoidable on such a project despite the best of protective clothing. For Vivian to work in no more than a bikini was asking for trouble, but if the trouble were serious, no rubber apron was going to make much difference. And in the humid, tropical heat, the constant wearing of seaboots and apron was less tolerable than the risk of minor injury, at least during daylight.

'I expect she'll take your concerns to heart once it cools off a bit tonight,' Jinx remarked, and turned away without waiting for a reply. Tonight would come soon enough, and she knew if she didn't grab what sleep she could, it would be a long and difficult experience.

Race made no comment, but she could *feel* his eyes following her as she manoeuvred her way along the deck. Damn the man! If he wanted to ogle Vivian—and what man wouldn't—that was fine with her. But at least he could have the decency to stay with one woman at a time!

Jinx went into the fo'c'sle to find Vivian right on her heels, her splendid body showing no ill effects of the day's work.

'I'm for a shower and then sleep,' said Vivian with a grin and a shake of her head to free her long hair from the confinement of the ponytail. 'You've got rank; want to go first?'

Despite her misgivings, Jinx couldn't help but like the other woman, and she replied with a grin of her own.

'There's only one rank on this boat, I think,' she said. 'You go on if you're ready; you did more work today than I did.'

'Skipper's getting to you already, I see,' Vivian observed with a directness Jinx found somewhat disconcerting. 'You'll have to watch yourself, or it's going to be a long, rough voyage.'

'I can take care of myself,' Jinx replied, keeping her voice calm, her attitude free of any hint of antagonism. There was, it now seemed, a chance she could work well with Vivian, and she knew she must maintain that chance as long as possible.

'You'll want to,' was the reply as Vivian turned away.

Jinx found herself pondering that brief remark through the long minutes until it was her turn in the shower, and it echoed in her mind as she splashed water over her body and sudsed the salt-spray from her tousled hair.

Did Vivian know something that she herself ought to know? Certainly, living in Darwin, the redhead would know far more about the authoritarian Captain Morgan than Jinx did, but her brief comment suggested something more, perhaps even something sinister.

She would have pursued the question further, but by the time she returned to the fo'c'sle everyone else was there, and Vivian was already asleep.

Nor was there any chance to bring up the topic during the work that night. Whatever else, Race Morgan knew his fishing, and when the nets went out after the early tropical night had fallen, everybody was far too busy for idle chit-chat.

The nets were shot, returned sagging with shark, the occasional tuna and mackerel, and both boat and scientific crews were busy straight through until dawn. By the time the tropical sun sprang from the sea ahead of them, everybody was too tired to care about its beauty.

With the exception of Race Morgan and Jinx, they were even too tired to care about breakfast. Gear was put away, a quick hosing of the deck sluiced the worst of the debris over the side, and everyone headed for the fo'c'sle in a shambling stream of weariness.

Jinx, too, was tired. But not sleepy, for some reason. She found the work exciting, exhilarating—hard, strenuous to be sure, but seldom exhausting, and certainly not now, not so early in the voyage.

Race Morgan didn't seem to notice the expenditure of energy, although he'd done as much physical work as anyone. He'd even, somewhat to Jinx's astonishment, taken a spell at helping her clear the nets of their writhing, snapping captives. When a particularly difficult hammerhead, a shark of well above average length and strength, had smashed him with a flailing tail, the captain had merely grunted with the impact, his own teeth bared in a shark's grin that seemed to challenge his twisting, fighting captive. Iron fingers sank into the shark's jaws; biceps bulged as he hugged the creature to him, swinging it towards the weighing table and Jinx's grasping fingers.

'Feisty little devil,' he growled through a triumphant grin as she struggled to hold the writhing shark's less dangerous end. 'Don't let go of that tail; he's already taken a chunk out of me.'

Jinx, surprised by the revelation, almost *did* let go, especially when she glanced down to see where a curtain of blood was slowly descending along Race's right thigh.

'Oh!' she cried. 'But you . . . you're bleeding badly! You've got to have treatment.'

'Just a scrape; I'll fix it up once we've got the little beggar tagged and measured,' he replied with a grin that seemed, to her frightened eyes, tinged with pain.

There was no arguing with him. When she tried again, he growled at her in a voice that snapped and crackled like an ancient pirate captain's cat-o'-nine-tails. She could only tend to the shark as rapidly as safety allowed, tagging it, measuring it, and making sure she kept a firm grip during its brief journey back to the rail and the warm Arafura Sea from whence it had come.

Then, however, she ignored Race's stoic appraisal of his injury and cried out for the net's progress to be halted.

'It's nothing,' protested Race. 'I'll just give it a wash while somebody else takes over . . . we've got a fair bit of net still to come in.'

'Damn the net!'

Jinx was angry now—angry with herself, angry with the unnecessary injury, angry with Race for doing the job in shorts and a pair of thongs after having criticised her for letting Vivian work in similar gear, angry for not having stopped both of them, for not having insisted on safety gear right from the start . . angry . . .

'You'll do as I say!' she snarled, peering up to meet his green-eyed, belligerent stare with a look that defied opposition. 'This is *my* part of the operation we're involved in now, *Captain* Morgan,' she said sternly. 'And that means if I say you get treatment immediately, that's what happens. No arguments, no chauvinistic rubbish, no rank-pulling.'

He grumbled, but it must have taken only a glance round the foredeck for him to realise that Jinx had the crew on her side. Both crews, in fact.

'We'll go to my cabin, then,' he agreed grudgingly, and stalked off, apparently oblivious to their audience.

Jinx followed, shaking now both from her anger and from the frustration of having to try to manage such an autocratic, infuriating man.

Once in his cabin, she found herself virtually redundant. Race had grabbed up a clean rag en route, and was already swabbing at the injury as he stalked through the door.

'What are you—my mother?' he growled as he turned to find Jinx behind him.

'What's that supposed to mean?' she wanted to know. 'It was you who said we'd come here, unless I remember wrongly.'

'You don't.' It was a grudging admission, helped not at all by the grimace as he splashed disinfectant across the raw patch on his thigh where the shark's abrasive hide had scraped away a square six inches of skin.

It must, Jinx thought, have hurt far more than the

original injury. She remembered Will Jacobs' home-made disinfectant . . . a mixture of standard brands and a particularly vile, pungent liniment that he swore would cure almost any ailment of man or beast. Will had been known to drink the liniment by itself to cure a cough, and on an open wound the mixture was like liquid fire.

But Race didn't so much as gasp when the burning liquid splashed across his bloodied thigh. He merely ripped off a length of dressing strip and wrapped it round his muscular leg, securing the dressing with a tight knot.

'It'll be right in a day or so,' he grunted, glaring at Jinx as if daring her to object to such rough-and-ready treatment. Both of them knew too well how easy it was to have a wound infect under tropical conditions, especially when dealing daily with marine organisms and primitive cleaning facilities.

'From now on, everybody will work in seaboots and aprons—including you!' she said sternly, knowing he would accept no arguments against his self-medication.

But she was half-way out of the door before logic struck like a blow between her eyes, and she turned to glare at him, thunderstruck by the mere thought of what she suspected.

His icy eyes returned her glare cat-like, without any readable expression. And although she knew he wouldn't satisfy her curiosity or even so much as admit that she might possibly have sussed out his thinking, she had to ask.

'It was . . deliberate . . . wasn't it?' she muttered, locking her glance to his, trying to fight though the sphinx-like silence of his stare.

'What *are* you on about?' he queried, but not until after a silence so long and so thick it seemed to hover like a tangible presence in the tiny cabin.

'You know very well what I'm talking about,' was all

she could reply. Then she turned away and slammed the door behind her, unwilling to give him any further satisfaction.

She plunged back to the working deck to find the net almost wholly rewound and a curious lack of curiosity on the part of the crew still assembled round the final catch of the night, a superb whaler shark that took three of them to subdue sufficiently for the tagging process.

Damn Race Morgan anyway, Jinx thought as she splashed from shower to bunk some half an hour later. He'd deliberately engineered the whole thing . . . and for what? To force her into doing what she should have done in the first place—insist on protective gear regardless of time or heat or circumstance.

And, she thought ruefully, to make sure Vivian's delicate skin was protected!

CHAPTER FOUR

JINX found little time during the next few days to worry about either her own motivations or those of Captain Race Morgan. The weather was good, the fishing even better, and everyone worked flat out to take every possible advantage.

As the boat moved steadily eastward across the top of Australia, they fished by long-line during daylight hours, by net during the relative coolness of the nights, and slept whenever they could find time in between.

By the time they sighted the Wessel Islands to the south and east, Jinx was certain her crew couldn't maintain the pace for much longer. And as they approached closely enough to actually see the vivid rocks that framed the Hole-in-the-Wall of Gugari Rip, she was almost too tired to appreciate the ruggedly vivid phenomenon. At a distance, the shorelines that framed the rip were merely impressive; from a closer vantage point they took on an aura of looming menace as they seemingly reached for each other across the narrow channel.

'You wouldn't think anybody'd be crazy enough to try and put a boat through there, would you?'

Race's voice was rough, unexpected as he leaned beside her against the bow rail. Jinx turned to look at him, but his gaze was focused on the natural phenomenon ahead. It was, she found herself thinking, almost as if he were assessing the rip, evaluating the risk, the challenge, and forming a mental assault. For now? Surely not, she thought, then found herself asking, 'You've done it, I presume?'

His laugh was harsh, almost angry. 'Where do you think all these grey hairs came from?' he replied, then added, 'But no, we're certainly not going to try and shoot the Hole-in-the-Wall . . . not today and I hope not ever.'

'But you said the prawn trawlers do it all the time,' she remarked, puzzled by the harshness of his reply, by the haunted look in his ice-green eyes as he spoke.

'All the time is a pretty broad generalisation,' he replied after what seemed an hour's silence. 'But yes, they do it fairly often. Doesn't prove anything except what I've always said . . . prawn fishermen are all mad idiots at the best of times.'

'And their boats are generally bigger than the *Perfidy*, of course,' Jinx mused, 'which must make a fair bit of difference.'

'All the difference in the world,' was the grim reply. 'To get through there in this boat, we'd need the tide and the wind with us and the luck of the devil to boot.'

Even as he spoke, the bow of the *Perfidy* was easing away to starboard as Dick French steered south-south-west to parallel the coast of Guluwuru Island.

'We'll go round through the Cunninghams, then start working our way down to Gove,' said Race, anticipating her question. 'Everybody's pretty well stuffed, so once we get into really sheltered waters we'll declare a holiday and see about getting a proper rest.'

'I don't think you'll find anyone to argue that plan,' Jinx replied. 'The fishing so far has been great, but it really is hard work.'

'Not as bad as I expected it to be,' was the somewhat surprising rejoinder. 'Both crews have fitted in well together.'

It was true, but the implied compliment was none the less unexpected, enough so that Jinx found herself unable to frame an immediate reply. Captured by Race's eyes and the hint of a grin on his generous, mobile mouth, she found herself gulping in a strained silence.

'Don't look so astonished,' he continued with what was now a maddening, exasperating grin. 'Don't tell me you're one of those people who can't handle even a simple compliment?'

'I . . . well, of course I can,' she stammered, thankful she could make that admission without having to own up to the fact that it was his nearness, his sheer physical presence that was the true cause of her confusion. The long, sloping shoulder muscles, the powerful, almost barbaric way he had of moving, and those damned *knowing* eyes . . . it just wasn't fair, she thought.

Because now, without her having mentioned a word of it, now he knew! He'd read her mind, or—like the predator he was—had just *sensed* her vulnerability.

His eyes formed a prison for her. She wanted to look away, *had* to look away, but couldn't. He could, she realised, simply reach out and take her, there and then.

And she saw in her peripheral vision the flexing of his strong fingers, the tensing of muscles in those sun-browned arms, felt her own tensing and knew it wasn't only fear. It was longing, too.

'We may have to do something about that some day,' he drawled, voice soft against the clattering of the engine, the soft swoosh of the waves against the bow.

Jinx didn't reply. There was nothing she could say that wouldn't just make the situation worse. Morgan, like the pirate she believed him to be, knew all too well the advantages he held, the power he subdued only because *he* wanted it that way.

Except . . . she found herself growing angry, suddenly. The sheer nerve of the man, the deliberate flaunting of his sexual appeal made her angry. No, not just angry. Furious!

'You can do something with it right now,' she snarled, eyes bright with her fury, hands clenching and unclenching at her sides as she forced herself to meet his sensual glance with her own anger.

'Such as?'

His voice was soft, almost gentle. And so damned . . . anticipatory. He'd sensed the challenge, welcomed it as he so obviously welcomed any challenge.

Jinx flared, 'In case you hadn't realised it, *Captain* Morgan, there are laws against sexual harassment!'

His grin flashed, silently at first. Then it erupted into a boom of laughter that seemed to light up his face.

'Not on my boat there aren't,' he finally said, voice soft and yet still rumbling with the humour he felt. 'On my boat, *Doctor* Beaumont, there are only my laws.'

'Well, then, you'd better plan on rigging up a brig,' Jinx snarled in reply, 'because I don't happen to think very much of your laws and in this particular area I don't plan to accept them at all. I'm my own person and I shall damned well stay that way!'

Which gained her, instead of the frowning assertion she had expected, only another boom of wicked, knowing laughter.

'I wouldn't have it any other way,' Race Morgan chuckled, though his eyes said he lied!

The captain's certainty of his own powers gave Jinx no cause for concern during the rest of that day, a day in which the *Perfidy* steamed south-west and then south into the protection of the Wessel group as it headed down towards the English Company's Islands and Cape Wilberforce.

The fishing pressure was slackened off; clearly Morgan had a destination in mind and was determined to reach it by early evening. He didn't actually say so, or at least not to Jinx, who was studiously avoiding him wherever possible, but everyone else on board also seemed to sense his mood, and no one questioned the increase in speed, the deliberate attention to his course.

And certainly no one complained when the *Perfidy* swung into a snug, delightful little cove late that afternoon and the boat's crew settled the anchors in the sand and coral bottom.

'Barbecue ashore in two hours,' Morgan announced, to cheers from both crews, cheers that were followed immediately by a lowering of the dinghy and a scramble for the commodities that would be needed.

Well before the sudden curtain of tropical darkness, masses of firewood had been collected and a fire blazed. The close-knit working habits from on board made organising the barbecue surprisingly simple. It was Jinx's turn to cook, and the change of venue didn't alter that. The boat's crew had things which had to be done, the scientific crew were delegated the establishment of a barbecue area, and all hands worked to ferry gear ashore and start preparations.

Morgan himself provided a shark and crocodile watch, then, while everybody else enjoyed the luxury of a swim in the warm, balmy waters shared with a myriad of brightly-coloured tropical fish.

To Jinx, floating on her back and struggling to hold back giggles as swarms of tiny fish nibbled at her hair, the imposing figure that prowled the deck of the boat above her needed only an eye-patch and a sabre to complete her mental picture of the arch-pirate she believed Race Morgan to be.

But that picture changed quickly when she raised her head to find that everyone else had swum ashore, and that Race had, inexplicably, disappeared. She looked around, surprised, then upward, to see him poised on the rail like a statue in teak. A living statue, clad only in the brief-

est of swimming trunks. And a living statue that suddenly
flew into the air and dived with exquisite grace and skill to
cleave the water only metres away from her.

In the crystal water, she could only watch as his
magnificent body slewed towards her, sliding through the
underwater world with the sleek grace of a true marine
creature. Then hands captured her waist and it was no
seal, no porpoise, but all too obviously a man whose
muscular body floated against hers, whose ice-green eyes
laughed into her own startled gaze.

'You shouldn't be swimming alone out here,' he said
with mock seriousness. 'Far too tempting if a shark or
croc should wander by.'

'You . . . you're supposed to be keeping watch against
that,' Jinx told him, struggling in total futility to keep him
from holding her body against the length of his own,
struggling to shut off her senses from the touch of his
muscled thighs, the warmth of him, the urge to throw her
arms around his muscular shoulders.

'Oh, but I am,' he grinned. 'A very close watch, in
fact.'

'Too close,' she gasped, wrenching herself free of his
embrace. 'And, if you don't mind me saying so—*Captain*
Morgan—breaking one of the firmest of ship's rules. Or
have you forgotten that there was to be absolutely no
swimming without a shark watch? None?'

'All the more reason for us to get ashore damned
quick,' was the enigmatic reply. 'Besides, I'm starving,
and it's your turn to cook, unless I'm mistaken.'

'Keep that up and you'll be in danger of being fed
toadfish,' she retorted, once again writhing against the
exquisite touch of his fingers about her waist.

She attempted to kick out at him, but could get no
purchase in the buoyant, salty water. What should have
been an assault became instead almost a caress as her

food slid ineffectually down the length of his leg.

Race only grinned in response, but the grin dissolved as Jinx cried out in shock and surprise at the stabbing pain of cramp that crinkled through her left calf muscle. Her eyes widened; the air seemed to have been driven from her lungs with the intensity of the pain. Her whole body seemed overcome with the need to fold up in a ball, to somehow alleviate the cramp.

Race, of course, knew immediately. 'Which leg?' he demanded, already reaching down with long fingers against the silky skin of her thighs. As she gasped a reply, he thrust her gently away from him, forcing her to lie back against the buoyancy of the sea as strong fingers kneaded the muscle, teasing out the knot, easing out the pain.

It seemed to take for ever, but in reality Jinx knew it was hardly a minute before the worst of the pain had gone. She grunted an order for him to stop, attempted to right herself, to begin the suddenly far too long swim to the pristine beach.

'Don't be stupid,' he growled, and again his fingers closed around her waist, holding her hard against him as he swam for the beach in a strong life-saver's kick.

Jinx attempted to protest, but she might as well have been half-drowned for all the notice he gave. Not until he was into shallow water where she could walk did he lower her, and even then he maintained his claim with a strong arm around her waist.

'I can walk by myself!' she said crossly, then nearly fell as he released her unexpectedly.

It was a temporary reprieve; his grip returned before the stumble was complete, and she had to endure the indignity of arriving at the campsite with his arm possessively clasped around her waist.

'Just cramp,' he drawled before anyone could do more

than look up with anxiety. 'I reckon our Jinx is one of those who shouldn't swim for an hour *before* eating, let alone an hour after.'

Jinx, finally given a chance to achieve proper balance, took the opportunity to spin herself clear of his grasp and immediately hobbled round to the far side of the small driftwood fire.

'It was nothing, really,' she denied. 'Probably just my stomach sending distorted messages or something.'

'I'll second that,' declared Dick French. 'Mine's doing something the same, so unless you're too maimed to cook I suggest you get at it.'

'I'm fine, really,' said Jinx, hobbling over to the impromptu kitchen and starting the preparations for dinner. Enormous steaks from the boat's freezer were already thawed, and some thoughtful soul had also brought ashore some fillets of fresh pomfret and various salad fixings.

An hour later, everyone was sprawling back in the sand, cans of beer in hand, lauding Jinx for her dab hand at open-fire cooking. Of the food, there wasn't enough left to feed a mouse, and all the rubbish had already been tidied up and either buried or burned in the now-dying fire.

'This is the life,' sighed Glen James. 'For two bob I'd be happy to stay here and let you pick me up on the way back again.'

'Two bob's worth of croc bait,' Race reminded him, his voice friendly but distinctively serious. 'You want to stay on this island, you'd want a bloody high place to hang your hammock at night, and lots of running room.'

'You're joking, surely,' said Glen, eyes widening as he realised immediately that Race definitely was *not* joking; he was being deadly serious.

'Sleep on the beach and find out,' the captain replied.

'Only wait until this voyage is over, because I wouldn't want to see us short-handed.'

'He's right, mate,' interjected Dick French. 'Since crocs became a protected species in 1971 they've bred like rabbits. There isn't a beach in the entire Northern Territory that *I'd* feel save sleeping on.'

'They can't be that much of a danger, surely,' argued Glen James. 'I thought they went on the protection list because they were almost wiped out entirely.'

'Almost is the word, and subject to a lot of interpretation at that,' said Race. 'I seem to recall seeing a television programme recently that estimated there are more than thirty thousand of them in the territory now. Of course,' he grinned mischievously at Jinx, 'that's a government estimate, and we know how inefficient the public service is. There could be thirty thousand or there could be sixty thousand; I doubt if anybody could provide truly accurate figures.'

Jinx ignored his sniping, as did the rest of her crew; Glen James found it more productive to continue quizzing Race about the reptile which carried prehistoric menace into modern times.

'Are they really as dangerous as we're led to believe?' he asked. 'I mean, the Aboriginals have lived with crocodiles for ever up here, and they don't seem to worry about them all that much.'

'Because they understand them, even worship them in places,' was the quiet reply.

'Worship them? You'd have to be joking,' scoffed Glen.

'Not at all, and I'd suggest if that's your attitude you'd best change it before we raise Gove,' replied Race. 'The Gumatj clan there has always had the croc as its totem, still does. If we've time there, you might want to see if you can have a look at the massive stuffed specimen the clan leaders have. There's quite a story behind that old devil.'

It took little urging from the now-interested audience to bring Race into the role of story-teller.

'There was a great flap there back in 1979 when a tourist got taken by a croc while spear-fishing below what they call Rainbow Cliffs,' he began. 'And in the resultant panic one big croc was killed and another taken alive.

'It was taken to the zoo in Darwin, but eventually it got sick or something and had to be destroyed. This didn't impress the Gumatj people all that much, as you might understand, but for once some government boffin got it right, and it was decided to stuff the animal and return it to the Aboriginals.'

'Stuffed?'

'Stuffed. It took more than five years, no less.'

'And then what?' This from Glen James, almost open-mouthed with interest.

'Oh, it was delivered among the usual pomp and ceremony,' Morgan told him. 'A wise political decision, for sure; the Aboriginals were as happy as they could be under the circumstances, and it made the administration look pretty good too.'

'Sounds a bit gimmicky to me,' said Glen suspiciously.

Race laughed, and the suspicion was matched by obvious cynicism.

'No more so than any other government public relations exercise,' he said before rising easily to his feet. 'And a distinct improvement over rushing out to shoot every croc in sight.'

Then, his attitude signifying that the discussion was over, he turned to reach down and hoist Jinx upright. 'You've still got a bit of stiffness in that leg,' he said quietly. 'Come on, we'll have a go at walking it out.'

The gesture and its attendant sympathy were so unexpected that she was on her feet and moving away

from the glowing fire before she could even think to
object. She allowed herself to be led along the moonlit
beach.

'And you won't have to worry about crocs here,' said
Race with a wry grin. 'They're about, of course, but
unless there's a female guarding a fresh nest back in the
scrub I doubt if one could sneak up on us in this light.'

'It isn't the crocs I'm worried about,' Jinx admitted
with a sideways, cynical glance of her own. Ahead, the
beach curved in a crescent of silver, lit by the brilliance of
the tropical moon so bright she could hardly believe it.

'That's hardly the attitude to take towards somebody
who rescues you,' said Race, his teeth flashing in a grin
that belied the danger she knew lurked behind it.
'Especially when you haven't so much as said thank you.'

'Thank you . . . I think,' she responded.

His grin widened.

'That's what I like, a person of enthusiastic responses,'
he chuckled.

They strolled for a time in silence then. Jinx was
content to do so, and her contentment was enhanced by
the fact that although he held her hand, there was no
move to intensify the degree of physical contact.

She couldn't deny—even to Race himself—his
attraction. But she didn't want to admit it either.

Fortunately, he seemed in no mood to try and force
such an admission, but appeared equally content to stroll
hand in hand, in silence, beneath the magic moon.

'Stiffness gone?'

The question, when it came, was like a wind whisper
against the thick tropical night, containing none of his
earlier aggression, none of his usual strong sexuality.

'Yes, I think so,' Jinx replied. 'I'm still a bit surprised
at having got a cramp in the first place, though. It . . . was
rather unexpected.'

'You forget what a strain being at sea can be,' was the curious reminder. 'You use different muscles, in different ways, to adjust to the motion and all. For you, the change from land-legs to sea-legs, and then to swimming, must have been a bit too much.'

'I suppose so,' she agreed, only partially aware that their progress had halted at the end of the curving beach. Ahead was only blackness as the sand gave way to the rock that formed the core of the island.

It was a strange feeling, far more curious than the cramp, to find herself so unexpectedly comfortable with Race Morgan. Too comfortable, really. Dangerously so.

She had a sudden urge to have his arm around her, to let her head rest against his muscular chest. Not in a sexual manner, but just . . . to be comforted, to be . . . held.

And as if he had once again read her mind, his fingers released her small hand, his arm lifting to encompass her shoulders, to draw her against him in exactly the way her fantasy had visualised. So gentle; so completely non-threatening. Jinx sagged against the hard warmth of him, sliding into a cocoon of exhaustion, a shroud of safety.

Neither spoke as they moved slowly back along the beach to where the remains of the campfire glowed like a tiny beacon of welcome. But as they drew within speaking distance of the others, Race eased away from her, seeming to ignore the unthinking mew of protest she uttered as his warmth and closeness was removed.

He said nothing, except to advise the crews that it was time to pack it in, time to climb into the dinghy and return to the *Perfidy*.

If anyone had noticed their close-knit arrival, no one said anything. Until the next morning!

'You realise you're letting yourself in for a lot of pain?'

The question, totally unexpected, came from Vivian Doherty. And it struck Jinx as severely as a physical blow, leaving her staring speechless at the statuesque redhead.

Both women were alone on deck while everyone else enjoyed a morning swim. Vivian was the designated shark watch; Jinx had wakened late, then decided not to risk her still-tender leg muscles.

'I . . . I really don't know what you mean,' Jinx said at last, feeling an inner anger building up at the other woman's unwarranted interference in her private life.

Especially after last night, a time which would float in her memory because of the warmth, the absolute melding of moods between herself and the volatile Captain Morgan. It was a time Jinx couldn't visualise being repeated for a long time—if ever—and she railed at having Vivian rain on her parade of memories.

'The hell you don't,' was the brutal reply. 'You know all too well what I mean.' Then the redhead's voice softened, unexpectedly, and she looked at Jinx through eyes that held no hostility, only empathy.

'Look,' Vivian sighed, 'it's none of my business and I know that, but please understand that I'm not trying to push you around. I actually quite like you, even though I certainly didn't expect to.'

'Well, thank you for that, I think,' said Jinx, and found herself having to admit, 'I quite like you too, and with the same proviso.'

Her quick grin was picked up by Vivian immediately, and she could feel the tension between them thaw and melt almost entirely away.

'Good,' said Vivian. 'So without putting that at risk, just let me say that I think you'd best be wary of our swashbuckling captain. I don't want to stickybeak into your business, but I've seen that man at work, and you're right out of your class. He eats girls like you for breakfast.'

'I hadn't intended to give him the chance,' Jinx said—and flinched inwardly at the sudden realisation that she was lying through her teeth.

She would give him the chance, and would give it to him any time, if she thought for one minute his attitude of the night would be repeated, if he showed feelings to match those of her own that she couldn't deny.

Vivian's response was perhaps predictable.

'Your story—you stick to it,' she said with a sad, slow shake of her auburn mane. 'Just don't forget that tropical cruises, even of our type, have an unreality factor that dies at the wharf when they're over.'

She turned away to scan the crystal waters of the tiny bay, then turned back to stare Jinx squarely in the eye.

'And don't forget the fair Melissa either,' she challenged. 'She may look like a Barbie doll, and sound even worse, but inside that juvenile façade she's as cunning an infighter as you'd want to meet. Worse than any shark or crocodile as far as you're concerned.'

'Very likely . . . if I were concerned at all,' Jinx told her with a wide grin and a shake of her own head. 'But I'm not, so why worry about it?'

'No reason at all,' Vivian grinned. 'Except that you're a lousy liar; really an amateur. Still . . . good luck!'

And I'll need it, thought Jinx as she wandered forward to the galley to get some breakfast before the rest of the crew returned.

Minutes later, she was surrounded by dripping, allegedly starving crew members. No more time to think.

The fishing resumed that afternoon as they steamed south again, headed round Cape Wilberforce towards Melville Bay and the Gove Peninsula.

Routine returned, as if their pause in paradise had

never happened; lines went out and came back, sharks of various sizes were wrestled to the hatch cover, measured, tagged, inspected. At night, the nets continued to produce good catches, and sleep became once again something to be snatched in short bursts, until they steamed up to the cargo wharf at Gove.

'Two days,' announced Race. 'And stay out of trouble or you'll answer to me.'

The warning was delivered with a stern look at Brian Roberts, who averted his own gaze, Jinx noticed, rather than meet the captain's stern, ice-green eyes.

She had somewhat the same problem, although for very, very different reasons.

'If you wouldn't mind waiting a bit, you and I can catch a cab into Nhulunbuy later,' said Race. 'I want to arrange for bait and fuel and whatever else we need before we head out for the bright lights.'

Jinx shrugged, no wiser for the lack of explanation about why her presence was required. Everyone else was busily showering and changing for their expedition into Nhulunbuy, the commercial and residential centre of the peninsula. The Gove Peninsula, she knew, had a unique situation, located in semi-isolatin at the north-eastern corner of the Northern Territory's Arnhem Land Reserve.

Its Aboriginal history went back to the Dreamtime; modern history of the region was an infant by comparison. Named for an Australian avaitor killed in the region during the second world war, and with the magnificent deep-water harbour of Melville Bay considered significant since Flinders' explorations of the early 1800s, the peninsula's major contributions in modern times were centred on tourism and bauxite/alumina production.

Even as Jinx waited for Race, the earliest on shore

leave had caught a bauxite bus en route to the town. The rest, she knew, would catch a lift or take a taxi as circumstances dictated. There was nothing much at the wharf to attrach their interest, as wharves, wherever their location, differed very little indeed.

And why, she wondered, had Race wanted her to stay back? He certainly didn't need her advice or involvement in the ordering of fuel and bait, or even whatever new foodstuffs that might be required.

She took the time to enjoy a leisurely, uninterrupted shower, changed into shorts and a light blouse against the fierce, humid tropical heat, then relaxed in a shady spot as she awaited Race's return.

He came up the gangplank in the easy, loping movement she had come to associate with the man, a wide smile revealing strong teeth and his eyes fairly dancing with some inner amusement.

'Right,' he declared as Jinx rose to meet him. 'Business all done. So tell me, young lady, what plans you had for this tropical paradise.'

'None, really,' she admitted. 'Just to go into the town, I suppose, and see whatever there is to see. Shake off my sea legs for a bit.'

'And what about food?' he demanded briskly. 'You know . . . that good stuff that for once nobody has to cook for everybody else?'

'I know what food is,' she assured him, casting her head to one side as she eyed him with growing suspicion. 'And I know there's a nifty hotel and a licensed club and all the mod cons here. What are you asking—if I'll forgo those in favour of eating aboard?'

It was a stupid question, and she realised that almost as soon as the words were out of her mouth, but if Race noticed, he gave no sign.

'I was asking if we could get together for dinner

tonight, obviously,' he said without taking her bait, without even indicating that he was aware of her sudden attack of nerves.

'I . . . well . . . I don't know,' Jinx found herself replying, and could have kicked herself for the instinctive uncertainty that forced such evasion. Of course she wanted to be with him; she'd have happily agreed to stay and cook for both of them, if he'd asked that.

But somehow, to dine in public . . . to do so with every chance some of the crew might be there . . .

'Is this a sudden show of modesty, or just your innate sense of caution where I'm concerned?' asked Race. And now his voice was taking on some of the 'captain' qualities so guaranteed to raise her own temper.

'All I'm saying is that I don't know what I'm going to be doing, where I'm going to be . . . when,' Jinx retorted—and then was forced to relent, forced by her own honesty. 'And—well, I'm not sure it would be such a good idea in such a small place,' she added rather lamely. 'The crew might—well, start getting the kind of ideas they shouldn't be getting.'

Race's laugh boomed across the deck, huge in its intensity, even larger in the streak of cruelty that flowed through it. When it stopped, it seemed to drive away even the echoes, even the vivid sounds of a busy, bustling harbour.

'Yeah,' he said at last. 'Yeah, I suppose so. OK, see you . . . whenever, I guess. We're sailing at dawn Tuesday.'

And he turned on his heel and stalked away to his cabin, not looking back, not appearing to hear Jinx's small sigh of despair at her own stupidity.

He must think her a child, or worse, she mused.

And later that day, once she'd realised just how small Nhulunbuy actually was, how often she came across Race

Morgan during her own unplanned wanderings, Jinx felt even more childish about the whole incident.

He turned up outside one shop where she was admiring some of the traditional Yirrkala bark paintings and carvings, but to her relief didn't pause in his own long, pantherish stride. When she paused for a cool drink at the Walkabout, he strode past—again without seeming to notice her—this time in the company of a tall, very slim man dressed in tropical whites.

She saw him three other times, luckily at a distance, during her roamings about the small community whose purpose in existence was almost solely due to the bauxite mining which had begun in the late sixties.

Jinx found the town fascinating, the region even more so because of its spectacular scenic location and relaxed life-style. If only she hadn't made such an utter fool of herself earlier, with Race Morgan, her day there might have been perfect.

She was back at the boat just before dark, debating her next move, when Vivian and Dick arrived.

'Get changed, get changed. It's almost party time!' they chorused, rushing into the fo'c'sle like a couple of mad teenagers.

'I'd say the party started a fair while ago,' Jinx told them with a shake of her short blonde curls. 'And I'm not sure I ought to . . .'

'Oh, stop being so stuffy,' Dick retorted. 'This is shore leave, for goodness' sake.'

'Yes,' added Vivian. 'What are you planning to do, spend the night in here all by yourself?' Then she added the crowning touch, as far as Jinx was concerned, by wondering aloud, 'Unless of course you're waiting for somebody?'

'Hardly,' Jinx shrugged. She didn't want to party, didn't think she was *capable* of partying the way

these rugged Territorians did, but equally certain she
didn't want to be alone for the evening. Or, worse, alone
when Morgan returned—if he did.

'Give me five minutes and the shower once you're
through,' she called to Vivian with a cheerfulness she
didn't really feel. It could only get better, she thought, not
realising how wrong her thinking could be!

CHAPTER FIVE

IT WAS more than a party—more like a travelling carnival, Jinx thought.

Typically Territorian, there was an element of utter craziness about the whole thing. She had once before seen such a performance, back in her days at university when there had been a brief fad for progressive dinner parties that switched venues for every course.

This party was vaguely similar in that it progressed through the residential area of Nhulunbuy, but equally dissimilar in that it was really a host of parties under a single banner.

At one house, heaps of seafood were the drawing card; at another it was the riotous music and dancing. A third seemed filled with tiddly philosphers who argued everything without conclusion.

People came and went without a semblance of pattern or order, all seeming to know instinctively which of the parties within the party would suit their mood best.

And wherever the action, Jinx's group of visitors was made abundantly welcome, overwhelmingly welcome.

Too welcome, she decided in the end. At every stop, the drink flowed in astonishing quantities. It was impossible to avoid drinking entirely; it seemed as if every second person considered themselves personally responsible for ensuring that everyone else's glass stayed full.

At the fourth stop, Jinx began to suspect she had acquired an admirer. By the sixth, she was certain of it, and not overly concerned.

The tall, slimly-built engineer who had finally been
introduced as Ted Mallanby was cheerful, good-
numoured and friendly without being at all threatening.
While he made much of Jinx, and was astonishingly quick
with his compliments, he made no move to try and
separate her from her companions.

Not so the second man who evinced an interest. This
one, a dark, stockily-built type with exotic, snapping dark
eyes, was far more quickly forthcoming.

'My name's Rick, and I fancy we should run away
together—preferably tonight!' was his opening line, one
fortunately rendered impotent by Ted's immediate
intervention.

'Go find your own lady, Rick,' he snapped before Jinx
could even think of a reply. 'If Jinx is going to run away
with anybody, it'll be me.'

'It'll be nobody,' she interjected, thus cutting short
Ted's explanation of why he, rather than the more
forward Rick, would make the best candidate for such a
venture.

It was obvious within moments that the two men knew
each other, were indeed drinking mates if not bosom
buddies, and had competed under such circumstances
before. Jinx played one off against the other, laughing
with both of them at the innocent pleasantries of the
game, and hardly noticing as the party moved on to yet
another venue.

At this house, blessed with a truly enormous outdoor
entertaining area, dancing was the order of the evening,
and Jinx quickly found herself entering into the spirit of
the thing. She danced with both men in strict rotation,
instinctively aware that it could be dangerous to give the
dynamic Rick any sense of advantage.

She danced, but all too quickly realised that she had
drunk too much wine, had not eaten enough of the

bountiful provisions heaped on tables all along the partying trail.

Her head began to spin, her balance awry, and she twice caught herself stumbling, lurching into Ted's quick grasp.

'Oh!' she muttered then in alarm. 'Oh, I think I'm going to have to sit down and rest a moment, if you don't mind.'

'Of course not,' was the smiling reply, and he steered her away from the outdoor area, moving through wide patio doors to a large room with proper couches and seating, and with tables piled high with tropical foodstuffs.

'I reckon you'd better eat something myself,' Ted said in concerned tones. 'Why not sit down here and I'll go rustle you up a plate.'

'Yes, thank you,' Jinx replied gratefully, slumping into the corner of a large, soft lounge, thankful for the subdued lighting in that corner of the room, even more thankful that the thudding sound of the outside music was muted here in the house, even if it still seemed to thunder inside her head. Suddenly she felt exhausted.

When Ted returned a few moments later with his friend Rick in tow and a plate heaped with prawns, oysters and various fruits, it seemed at first as if Jinx would become the focal point for yet another stage of the men's rivalry. But Ted, apparently the more empathetic of the two by far, firmly steered his mate away, correctly reading Jinx's need to just be alone for a time.

'We'll catch up with you after you've eaten,' he said with an understanding smile. Jinx matched it, watched the two men head off towards the bar, then closed her eyes for a moment as she gathered strength for an assault upon the plate of food in front of her.

The food was splendid. The enormous king prawns

were icy cold and succulent, the sauce to go with them
suitably tart and delicious; the chilled oysters had their
own special sauce, different from that for the prawns but
somehow quite complementary. And the fruit, so
obviously fresh and locally produced, removed any need
for a drink to help wash down the food.

Replete, Jinx moved to set the empty plate on a side
table, then returned to her corner and once again slumped
into the lounge, her eyes casually sweeping the room.
Safely obscure in her corner, she watched people enter the
room, glance almost secretively about, then load their
plates to overflowing with the succulent seafoods and
other delicacies. It was, she decided with a wry smile,
almost as if they were all diet-breakers, ashamed of their
gluttony but helpless to break the habit.

For her own part, she thought a return to the boat
might well be in order; she'd had enough of partying for
one night. Jinx's thoughts coincided with a realisation of
just how comfortable the lounge was, especially since she
had kicked off her high-heeled, sling-back shoes and lifted
tired feet to stretch out with her head supported by the
arm-rest.

The next visitors to the heaping trestle tables passed
slightly out of focus. The ones after that, she didn't see at
all. Her eyes had succumbed to her weariness, and within
minutes she was happily asleep, the party noises muted by
her exhaustion.

'You reckon we ought to wake her?'

The words sifted through to Jinx's consciousness,
stirring her into a half awake/half asleep condition.

It wasn't until she'd somehow identified the second
voice, the growly one that sounded like something being
dragged across gravel, that her eyes flew open in disbelief
and embarrassment.

'If she isn't awake by the time the party's over here,

I'll make sure she gets back to the boat,' Race Morgan had said, and there was an element of disappointment or anger in his words that shocked her awake.

'I'm quite capable of finding my own way back,' she retorted in the midst of thrusting herself upright to face her captain and—surprise, surprise—an immaculately turned out Melissa Stewart. The blonde had been poured into a lime-green cat-suit that revealed to all possible advantage that infuriatingly perfect figure, and her long hair was allowed to flow with studied casualness down her back.

Jinx, her mouth tasting sour from sleep and her mind flurried with embarrassment, could only feel dowdy by comparison, which did nothing for her composure.

Melissa's attitude was predictably condescending and disdainful, but Race Morgan seemed outright hostile, although Jinx couldn't reason why. There was a hint of a sneer on his sensuous mouth as he stood glaring down at her as if she'd been caught with her fingers in the till.

'Well, you'd best get started before you pass out again,' he growled, and turned on his heel to start walking away, so that Jinx's reply could only be directed at his broad, departing figure.

'I was *not* passed out!' she hissed, her mind throwing daggers right between those muscular shoulders.

If he heard, Race gave no indication of it. He was already three-quarters of the way across the room, and moving with such determination that he clearly wouldn't be distracted by the display of exotic foods he was passing. Melissa, however, quite clearly heard the retort, and the pseudo-sympathetic glance she threw to Jinx, like a bone to a stray dog, fairly reeked of patronising superiority.

'Bitch!'

The word slipped out unbidden, but was bitten off so quickly that neither Race nor his companion could hear.

Jinx was on her feet, half determined to follow them, to demand that Race listen, then thought better of it.

To hell with him . . . with both of them, she thought. She'd return to the boat when she was good and ready, and now wasn't the time.

Instead, after sliding on her shoes, she made a trip to the powder room for a full-scale repair job on her hair and make-up. Then she stalked back to the party, her back rigid, her eyes fiery and bright with a challenging anger.

Across the patio. she could see Race and Melissa dancing closer than morality should allow to a slow, intimate number that seemed vaguely familiar. Of Ted and Rick, admirers she would now welcome, there wasn't a sign.

Jinx cast a predatory eye across the crowd, hoping there would be some available man to help her counteract Race's damnable interference, but, finding none, she turned instead to the bar. Moments later she was perched on a high bar stool, a glass of Riesling in her hand, her mind finally beginning to work on its own behalf instead of through the channels of sheer rage.

What was Melissa doing here? Surely her arrival must have been unexpected, considering Race had asked *her* to dinner only hours earlier?

Just as well she'd put him off, Jinx thought to herself. Otherwise . . . she stifled a giggle at the thought of her captain having to explain away a change of plan that would have given *her* the upper hand, just for once.

She grinned to herself, wondering how he'd react if she didn't return to the boat at all that night. Then the grin soured. He probably wouldn't even notice, presuming he himself returned. And would he have the gall to bring Melissa back to share his cabin, knowing his crew were only a few feet away?

Jinx frowned, more at the shiver such thoughts sent

scurrying down her spine than at the morality or lack of it which might be involved. Young Melissa might be, but she was certainly old enough to handle such a situation without Jinx's consideration.

'What business is it of mine, anyway?' she muttered to herself, throwing back the contents of the wine glass and leaning across to refill it from the party-pack wine cask that shared the bar-top with dozens of others.

An hour later she hadn't moved, despite increasingly sour glances from her captain when he deigned to notice her.

Jinx was fully enjoying herself now. The wine had gone to her head, combined with a surprisingly thorough savegeness. She couldn't imagine why Race Morgan was so thoroughly miffed with her, or even why he should trouble to notice her at all.

But if he did—and it was his choice, not hers!—then she felt fully entitled to delight in his discomfort. Why indeed he hadn't taken Melissa off to his boat long before, Jinx didn't know and didn't care. It suited her to play up his darkening scowls, even if she wasn't entirely certain of her own motives.

She thought, once or twice, about leaving this particular venue in favour of somewhere new, somewhere where there would be more single people, less of a romantic, slow-music atmosphere. But each time, such thoughts were distracted by a flash of Race Morgan's ice-green eyes, eyes that seemed to stab across the width of the room and yank at Jinx's attention.

Once she saw him turn towards her, and she shrank back against the bar, instinctively shying from the patent anger she could read on his face. And once she found herself wishing he would approach, perhaps even ask her to dance. She thrust that thought away.

Other men asked her, and she was sort of tempted. But

only sort of. It was, she decided, far more pleasurable to lounge against the bar, her wine cask handy, and sip at the cool Riesling while watching Race Morgan through half-closed eyes. He was so devilishly attractive, the more so because of the increasingly angry scowls he was sending her way, Jinx thought—and wondered what could be provoking his anger.

Surely he couldn't be angry with her simply for being at the party? Much less, she thought, for being at the particular venue he was visiting with the luscious and lascivious Melissa?

'And besides,' she muttered to herself beneath her breath, 'I was here first.'

She looked across at where Race and his young companion continued to dance, so close to each other as to give the impression of being almost one body, then looked down at the floor.

When she raised her eyes again, there was no longer the dazzling reflection from Melissa's cat-suit, but across the room she could see Race Morgan turning towards her, awesome determination readable in his eyes.

'Come for a drink, captain?' Jinx asked as he slowed to a halt before her, glowering down from his full height like some mobile thundercloud.

'No, I've had enough,' he replied, leaving unspoken his obvious opinion that Jinx had imbibed *more* than enough.

'You're sure? It's really quite nice,' she said, ignoring his stern disapproval as she turned to refill her glass.

A strong, darkly tanned hand shot forward, fingers clawed as if to snatch the glass from her grasp. Then it paused, hovering malignantly, before Race returned the claw to his side without saying a word.

Jinx smiled to herself, but when she'd filled the glass and looked back at him, she reduced the grin to one of mere politeness and fearlessly met the challenging hostility in his gaze.

'I really do think you've probably had enough,' he said, the words emerging through gritted teeth in a futile attempt to maintain some credence of polite disinterest.

'Perhaps,' she agreed with a broad smile. 'But then again, perhaps not. After all, who knows where I might end up after this? And I'm not driving.'

'I should hope not,' was the soft-voiced reply, soft and yet somehow alive with a tension that sang through his words like an over-sized tuning fork.

'Should you?'

Jinx's grin was purely internal now, purely for herself. She felt that for once she had the mighty Captain Morgan on the defensive, and she ws determined to keep him there as long as she could manage it.

The arrival of Ted Mallanby, fortunately unaccompanied by his mate Rick, she met with a cry of delight.

'How wonderful, Ted! I've just been waiting for that dance you promised,' she purred, and without bothering to introduce the two men, she slid off the bar stool and into the arms of a slightly bemused but none the less game Ted Mallanby.

She could feel Race's eyes like laser beams as she spun around the dance-floor, far more closely in Ted's grasp than she would normally have accepted. She had no idea what effect her behaviour might be having on the piratical captain, but if it was somehow upsetting him, that was prize enough.

More than enough!

Somebody had obviously determined to lighten the romantic mood of this particular party segment, and the music was far more active than when she had been watching Race and Melissa in their seductive coupling.

Now the music became faster still, and after a few minutes on the floor with Ted, there was yet another change to outright, old-fashioned rock-'n'-roll.

Jinx was pleased; she had already half regretted letting herself go quite so far, and now had visions of a battle in getting rid of Ted once he had served his purpose. She had no intention of getting any further involved with him than this particular party, and was starting to get small guilty twinges about having so blatantly taken advantage of his good nature.

As they broke apart to dance facing one another, the harsh rock music thudding from the rafters, Ted grinned at her with an expression that showed just how obvious her strategy must have appeared.

'It isn't going to work, you know?' he asked, voice only just reaching her over the roar of the music. And then he grinned at her expression of curiosity. 'It won't . . . not with Race Morgan.'

'I don't know what you mean,' protested Jinx, but she did it with a broad grin of her own, realising immediately the futility of playing the innocent. Ted obviously knew her captain, and despite the wine she'd drunk, she realised that only a fool could have missed the byplay between Race and herself.

'You know exactly what I mean, but you can deny it if you want to; I don't care,' was the grinning reply. 'Just remember, pretty girl, that if Race Morgan decides to stack on a blue over this, I'll be the first bloke out of the firing line, that's all.'

'Stack on a blue? But why should he want to start a fight? And about what?'

Jinx was being deliberately, almost provocatively obtuse. She knew that Ted understood exactly what was going on, or at least enough that he'd already decided to limit his involvement.

'Besides,' she grinned with a devilish look back over her shoulder to where Race was once again dancing with Melissa, 'I should think he's got quite enough on his plate . . . don't you?'

'Wonder if he'd trade places,' was Ted's reply.

'Now that,' said Jinx, 'is hardly a gentlemanly thing to say.'

'And it wasn't accompanied by any gentlemanly thoughts either. I can assure you of that,' Ted assured her, then laughed.

An instant later, his laughter faded and there was a strange, almost fearful light in his eyes. 'If you don't want trouble, I'd suggest an immediate retreat to the powder room,' he warned. 'No need to say who's coming, although I'm sure you know better than I do what he wants.'

Jinx froze, thus losing the few seconds vital to any dignified, reasonable escape.

'May I?' growled an all-too-familiar voice, and she didn't even hear Ted's words of assent because she was being spun about into a grip like iron, her eyes instantly caught by an ice-green, fiery gaze.

And as if by magic, the music changed from raucous rock to a slow, much-too-intimate mood theme that gave Race any excuse he might have needed to pull Jinx in against his vital, muscular body and twirl her in slow, sensuous circles that quickly spun the wine to her head as if in a centrifuge.

And he knew it, the scheming devil!

Jinx found herself catching fleeting glimpses of Ted as Race deliberately spun her around, but all the help she was offered from that quarter was a wry grin and a glance that told her she was totally on her own.

Not a word from Race; only fingers that played a tune along her spine as he held her entrancingly close, crushing her breasts against his mighty chest, forcing her pelvis against him, defying any attempt to put distance between them.

Never before had Jinx prayed for a dance to end, for a piece of music to somehow self-destruct. She found herself sending useless mental messages to Ted, pleading with him to pull the plug on the record player, to short-circuit the house's wiring, anything to give her an instant's respite, a chance to draw a breath, to think . . .

'You're bound and determined to fight me, aren't you?' asked a gravelly voice near her ear. A voice that throbbed with too many emotions, too much passion, too much threat.

Jinx didn't reply, couldn't reply. For one thing, he was holding her far too tight; for another, she suddenly didn't trust herself to speak!

'No arguments? My goodness, that's something of a surprise.' His voice, alive with sarcasm, purred into her ear like that of some great predatory cat.

'I . . . I really don't understand what you're on about,' Jinx finally managed to reply. 'This is a party, that's all. I didn't come here to fight with you; I didn't even know you'd be here.'

Nor, she said without saying it, and realised he must catch the implication, who you'd be with.

'And that's the excuse for behaving like a deckhand?' The voice was still purring, but now it held a tinge of a growl that couldn't quite offset the somehow gentle warmth of his breath against her ear and neck.

'I was not!'

Jinx tried to push herself away from him, to gain sufficient breathing space to assert herself. It was like pushing against a solid brick wall.

'OK.'

He made no move to release her, even less to explain the sudden, unexpected acceptance of her denial. It was so surprising that it took a moment for her to realise the music had stopped but Race's embrace had not.

Where was Melissa? That was her first thought; the second was a renewed struggle to free herself from the heady closeness of his grasp.

Then, all too soon, the music resumed and it was too late. Morgan had her enslaved, their bodies moving as one in time with the slow, haunting melody.

Jinx couldn't help herself. The wine, the days of strain, the sheer magnetism of the man himself—all combined to conquer her. She slid from a mood of cranky agitation to one of light-headed acceptance, moulding her body to his wishes, her feet to follow his lead, her head suddenly soft against his shoulder.

Madness! But even as she knew it, the knowledge was too late; her body was no longer her own, her mind had switched off all objections, was now lost in rhapsody. Again she failed to realise it when the music in the room halted, because the music inside her went on and on and on.

The end came like a hosing down with ice-water. For whatever reason, the music they had been dancing to once again switched to hard, driving rock, and Race stopped dancing so quickly that Jinx stumbled, almost knocking both of them over.

'Sorry about that, but this isn't my taste in dancing at all,' said Race, but there was no real sense of apology in that gravelly voice. There was, instead, some element Jinx couldn't identify; a remoteness, almost.

He was escorting her back towards the seating area when she realised the reason. Melissa, shimmering like some modern neon statue, was leaning against the bar watching them, her eyes like ice, her smile so far from welcoming that Jinx felt a shudder down her own spine.

'So nice of you to keep Race occupied while I was . . . busy,' the blonde cooed, and the lack of any response from her captain brought Jinx to her own icy reply.

'All part of the job,' she said with a cold smile of her

own and without another word she turned away, afraid to
look at Morgan, even more afraid to continue this verbal
duel with his girlfriend.

Ten minutes later she was meeting a taxi outside on the
footpath, her heart numb but her mind working overtime as
she tried to decide about returning to the boat or instead
taking a room at the motel, where her privacy would be
assured regardless of what Race might decide.

The motel won, but only in the short term.

Jinx slept like a rock, only to find herself wide awake and
clear-headed at the crack of dawn. Her system was so used to
the irregular hours on the boat that it had easily absorbed the
abuses of too much wine, too much dancing and not quite
enough sleep; the merest hint of searing tropical sunlight and
she couldn't have slept a moment longer if she'd wished to.

And now . . . a whole day with nothing to do but whatever
she wanted. She would have to sleep aboard the *Perfidy* that
night, considering that Race's concept of a dawn sailing
might be highly suspect, but this day—all of it—was entirely
her own.

She would, she decided, begin with a swim in the motel
pool. It would clear her head, give her an appetite for
breakfast and maybe even help her to put last night's
bewildering experiences into some kind of perspective.

Minutes later, alone and relishing her solitude, she was
lazily coursing through lengths of the pool, her mind solidly
gnashing at the circumstances of the night before.

Why had Race been so obviously angry with her, then so
quick to accept her defence? And how had he so easily
conquered her on the dance floor?

It was disconcerting, to say the least. She had never
denied, even to herself, that Race Morgan was a most
impressive specimen of male animal. Nor that he held a
certain personal attraction for her, though she wasn't certain
at all whether it was purely physical or held something

else that—for the moment, anyway—she just didn't want to face.

She didn't even bother to try and work out Melissa's place in all this. It was, she thought, patently obvious. Nor did she try to reconcile her own reaction to the stunning blonde. They had instant antipathy, no two ways about it, and nothing she could imagine would change that.

But was it because of Race? Because of Jinx's own unspoken and unaccepted feelings for the captain? She didn't know, and refused to think about it long enough to find out. Better, she thought, to endure the remainder of the voyage without further involvement, catch the plane back to Hobart, and try to forget Race Morgan as quickly as possible. He was far too volatile a personality, far too much man for her to be messing with.

She left the pool and sprawled out on a lounger to dry off, eyes closed and mind surging unreasonably.

Damn the man anyway! Try as she would, Jinx couldn't find any explanation for his contradictory behaviour, much less for her own. And try as she would, she also couldn't deny his attraction. Before her short-cut wavy hair was dry, she'd found herself half admitting to an element of jealousy about Melissa, and sneering at herself because of the totally unwarranted bitchiness.

There was no reason for it, she told herself. Race Morgan had given her no reason whatsoever to question his relationship with Melissa or anyone else. His attitude towards herself had either been antagonistic or overbearingly macho. Except, she remembered, as they danced.

Sighing, she turned over and lay face down, feeling a gentle breeze across her back, soft tendrils of tropical wind lapping up the beads of moisture from her body. Her eyes closed, then opened as a shadow blocked the sun from her shoulders and she heard, simultaneously, the splash of someone diving into the pool behind her.

No poured-into trouser suit this morning. Melissa was instead poured into what might have been called a bikini in some parts of the world, but to Jinx's mind was no more than a few narrow bands of material. And her body it revealed was so startlingly, icily perfect that she could hardly refrain from a catty sigh of despair. Black, obviously of foreign design, and so close to being non-existent it wasn't funny, and yet the pseudo-swimsuit was perfect for Melissa. It complemented her youth, the perfection of her figure, the unquestionable beauty of her face and that mane of blonde hair.

But it did nothing for her voice, much less the sibilant, almost hissing aggression that was aimed directly at Jinx.

'If I didn't know better, I'd think you were following me, which would be a very stupid move, if you get what I mean,' Melissa began.

She got no further. Jinx was already on her feet, fighting for control as she started away.

'Don't flatter yourself; you're hardly my type,' she heard herself retorting, the words emerging without direct thought, without conscious planning. The reply was almost an instinctive defence, revealing in startling clarity how basic, how inborn was the antipathy between the two women who hardly knew each other.

Jinx suddenly found herself face to face with such hatred, such anger, that she could hardly believe it. Melissa towered about her, seeming to grow with the madness in her blazing eyes, to hiss even more serpent-like.

'You . . . you'll be sorry for that!' the blonde snapped, each word spat out like something foul. 'You'll pay—I'll make sure of that. And you won't like the price!'

For an instant, Jinx stood transfixed, totally astonished at the vehemence emerging from this child. And child Melissa was, she realised. A nasty, vicious, perhaps *dangerous* child in a woman's body.

She saw Melissa's hands curling into taloned claws, sensing the attack before it came. And without thinking the matter through, knowing there was no time for that now, Jinx half turned away. She didn't want a fight—had trouble, in fact, believing that a physical attack from Melissa was not only possible, but probable.

She stooped quickly to reach for her towel, and it was that sudden movement that saved her as Melissa's long, sharp nails slashed across where Jinx's face had been an instant before.

The suddenness of the attack was frightening, now.

Jinx felt herself trapped. Before her, a girl quite obviously mad, or drugged, or . . . whatever. A vicious, demented girl who meant business in her attack. Behind her, the cluster of deck chairs and loungers made escape a problem; one slip, one collision with the poolside furniture, and she'd be in real trouble.

Instinct saved her. Bracing herself with one hand on her own lounger, she used the other to snap the towel hard towards Melissa's face, cutting off the second slashing attack.

She was stunned, her defence clumsy in the face of such an unexpected and vicious assault. Indeed, her mind was still in shock when her body twisted, her shoulders thudded down on the pool surround as her feet caught at Melissa's legs, tipping the girl untidily to one side—and into the deep end of the pool.

Melissa's snarl turned to a squeal of outrage as the slender, splendid body struck the water, but Jinx heard only the snarl. Before the splash had settled she was on her feet and fleeing, her mind numb at the implications of the encounter. Not until she reached the safety of her room did the shakes begin.

CHAPTER SIX

IT WAS an hour before Jinx could stop shuddering and face her wild-eyed image in the mirror. Longer still before she had come to terms, even partially, with what had happened.

At first it had seemed unbelievable, impossible. She had never been attacked by another female in her entire life, much less retaliated physically!

At one moment she found herself giggling hysterically at the thought of having kicked Melissa into the pool, but a moment later the sobering truth of the assault had tears forming in her shock-widened eyes.

'It's like something out of a bad movie,' she heard herself saying aloud.

And then, 'The child is quite mad. She must be!

And, 'Does Race know this aspect of her? Dangerous!'

Her hunger, enhanced at first by her swim but then as swiftly dissipated by the unexpected assault, returned with a vengeance. But Jinx couldn't face the thought of encountering Melissa in the motel restaurant.

'Or anywhere else, for that matter,' she muttered, reaching for the room service phone. Far more sensible to breakfast in her room, she thought, and when it was time to leave, she'd ensure that a taxi was waiting at the door.

As she worked her way through a platter piled high with bacon and eggs, toast and fresh tropical fruits, she deliberated with her conscience about whether or not to mention the incident to the captain.

'If I don't, and she does, I'm in trouble,' she muttered around a mouthful of food. 'And if I do and she doesn't, I'm in just as much.'

What to do?

Over her second cup of coffee, she decided it was most likely nobody would mention the incident. It had happened without witnesses, discounting the unseen person who had dived into the pool before the attack began.

And with that thought came panic. Had the unseen swimmer, perhaps, been Race Morgan himself?

Jinx found herself gasping, and not from the heat of the coffee. It was, she decided, not only possible but quite likely. Morgan would not have taken Melissa back to the boat after the party, but he might very well have taken her to a tryst at the motel. And if he had . . . and if *he* had been the only possible witness to the ludicrous assault . . .

'Oh, to hell with it!' she muttered. 'If it was him, he'll only put his own interpretation on the whole thing anyway, and if it wasn't . . . well . . .'

Twenty minutes later she was packed, the cab was called, and she found herself in the process of checking out. Melissa, fortunately, was nowhere in sight. Nor was the blonde at the boat when Jinx arrived after the short drive across the peninsula. Indeed, the boat was deserted, which Jinx thought might be just as well. She was in no mood to have to try and be nice to anyone just at the moment.

Stowing her gear, the party clothes returned to their travel bag, she trudged in bare feet to the upper deck and sprawled in a deck chair in the shade. In her brief shorts and halter, she drew her share of whistles from passing vessels, but ignored them.

She lounged about, deep in formless thought, until nearly lunchtime. Her mind seemed to be floating like seafoam, unable to reach a viable decision, unable to even fully work out the implications of the morning's incredible incident.

Unwilling to return to town—she'd seen virtually everything worth seeing in the shopping complex, she decided—Jinx voted instead to prepare a light salad for

lunch and then spent the afternoon bringing her records up
to date.

It was, she decided, easier to immerse herself in the
repetitive work than to resume being a tourist while her
mind was dreading a confrontation with the unfathomable
Race Morgan, whose return to the boat she dreaded more
with each passing hour.

When he did return, however, she was so deep in
concentration that she didn't even realise he was standing in
the galley entrance until she happened to look up and see
him there.

'Funny way to spend shore leave,' he said, muscular body
not moving from its balanced poise above bronzed,
muscular legs.

He was wearing his usual gear—tropical white shorts and
singlet—which Jinx immediately took to mean that he had
returned to the boat at some time between the party and her
arrival earlier in the day.

At the party, he had been suavely, dangerously handsome
in a lightweight tropical suit, knitted tie and shoes that had
gleamed with polish. But this, she couldn't help thinking,
was the *real* Race Morgan. Still neat, tidy, shipshape, and
yet so undeniably masculine, almost piratical in his fiercely-
chiselled features, that salt-and-pepper, steel wire hair.

All he needed was a crimson sash round his waist and a
sabre in one capable fist, she thought, then realised she'd
been staring, his question unanswered.

'It's got to be done some time,' she shrugged. 'And I've
had enough sightseeing, I guess.'

'You certainly couldn't have seen everything just during
yesterday,' was the ambiguous reply. Race didn't move;
simply stood in the doorway like some rigid combination of
man and statue.

'Enough to know that if I went back into town today, I'd
only end up spending money,' Jinx replied tightly.

'And that's so bad? I'd bet money you haven't bought so much as a single souvenir.' Still enigmatic, still unsmiling, and yet, Jinx thought, not quite unfriendly.

'Not even a postcard,' she replied, then looked away as her memory betrayed her. She *had* her souvenir of the Gove Peninsula, she realised. It was the memory, etched into her mind with indelible, photographic intensity, of that final dance with this man, a dance in which she had felt them melding, fusing together. Or was that only *her* memory, her own interpretation of something that had meant little if anything to Captain Race Morgan?

He shrugged, then, before stretching like a massive, powerful cat. His eyes roved across her own, then down to take in the revealing costume. Jinx felt herself shrinking from that gaze, until she remembered the flimsy swimsuit that Melissa had worn—had it been only that same morning? With that, she sat up straighter and met his glance with fierce determination.

'Nobody to send even a postcard to? That's a bit rough, isn't it? Not the boss? Not the boyfriend?'

He was fishing, and Jinx found herself unable to keep from the bait.

'I wouldn't send my boss a glass of water if he was dying in the desert,' she replied fiercely, then shut her mouth before she could add that there wasn't any boyfriend.

Race, if he noticed the omission, ignored it.

'There'll likely be no chance to send anything after we leave in the morning,' he muttered. 'Or at least not until we're back in Darwin again.'

'Which will be when?' asked Jinx, not really that interested, but taking safety in the neutrality of the conversation.

He shrugged. 'Another week; another fortnight. Maybe even longer, depending on the weather and how your studies go. Why, does it matter?'

'Not to me,' Jinx replied. 'I'm certainly in no hurry to return to a Hobart winter.'

'Not something I'm familiar with,' Morgan said. 'In fact, I've never seen real snow in my life; only on the telly or in the movies.'

'It isn't anything you can't do without.' Jinx couldn't help smiling at just how this sunbronzed northerner might react to the icy blasts of snow and wind that crowned Hobart's Mount Wellington during winter.

Race advanced into the room, seating himself across the galley table from her before he continued the discussion.

'And I suppose you get all involved in skiing and winter bushwalking and all that sort of thing?' he asked, evincing a show of interest Jinx found most surprising.

She grinned again. 'Not on your life,' she told him. 'As far as I'm concerned, winter in Hobart is marvellously sunny, crisp days and nights in front of the fireplace. I think snow is lovely to look at—from a distance—but I could live without it quite happily.'

Race's eyes seemed to narrow in a brief jolt of speculation, and this was borne out by his next comment. 'You should like it up here, then.'

It wasn't quite a question, but there was an element of fishing there somewhere, and Jinx thought carefully before replying.

'Oh, I do. Although I'm not all that keen in the wet season. Rain that never seems to stop can be just too depressing. And I think I'd prefer snow to cyclones, if you really want to get picky about it. Actually it's just about impossible to compare Tasmania to the Territory.'

'Difficult to compare the Territory to anywhere in the world, except perhaps part of north Queensland,' Race agreed with a half-grin of his own. 'Sometimes I wonder if we haven't made our own legend up here, with a bit too much of it stolen from American cowboy movies.'

'It is still something of a frontier,' Jinx suggested, now fishing a bit herself, trying to keep him talking. It seemed this was the first time she'd ever found Race prepared to discuss his chosen home in anything except the broadest general terms, and she, for whatever reasons, was suddenly vitally interested.

But it wasn't to be. His interest in the discussion seemed to vanish as suddenly as it had come.

'Better you finish your paperwork. I've got bad vibes about the weather that's coming, and this may be the last chance you have for a bit.'

And he was on his feet and moving out of the narrow galley without waiting for any reply from Jinx, who found herself wondering, even more than usual, just what made Captain Race Morgan tick. The weather this afternoon was perfect Territory weather for the season, and nothing on the noon forecast had predicted any change.

She waited a moment, then followed out to the deck in time to see Race striding off down the wharf. Jinx looked up to a sparkling blue sky with only wisps of light cloud and only the beginnings of a gentle breeze.

She wondered again at his 'bad vibes', especially when the weather remained clear and sunny right through to the arrival of the swift tropical night. As the other crew members arrived from their shore leave, she waited to hear other comments about the weather, but their minds were clearly on other things.

Nor did Race mention it again at dawn.

They were all up early, and cast off from the wharf just as the sun lofted into the sky as if shot by a catapult from somewhere in the sea to the east.

It was a far different departure from their earlier one from Darwin. Now the crew worked as a team; all the wrinkles were removed from their efforts and they left Melville Bay on a northerly course beneath cloudless skies and over a gentle swell.

Race stayed in his cabin most of the day, leaving the work on deck to those already assigned it. Occasionally the sound of the chattering radio made it clear he was in contact with other vessels, but he said nothing to Dick French or the other crew members.

That night they were fishing near the Malay Road, and by morning it was clear Race was embarking on an unusual change of direction. Jinx waited until noon the next day for him to bring up the change, then took her courage between her teeth and braced him about it.

To her surprise, he took her question with remarkable calm, even to the extent of grinning before he replied. He had obviously been expecting her to enquire, she realised.

'I'm still dodgy about the weather,' he said, 'and yes, I know there isn't a single reason to be.'

True enough, unless his radio work had turned up something their own observations couldn't determine. The sky was still clear and blue, the breezes gentle and totally without any legitimate sign of threat.

But Race Morgan's instincts were giving him some different message, and on that alone he had changed course to bring them into sheltered waters off Inglis Island. Given time, he explained, they would seek even better shelter in the entrance to Arnhem Bay.

It was clear to Jinx that nobody else in the crew was about to question his logic—or lack of it. And her own instincts protected her from doing anything different. If seamen like Dick French and the mountainous Tiny had faith in Race, it would be the height of amateurism for her to show less. Not that she would be so inclined. If anything, she thought, her own faith in Race's instincts might even exceed that of his crew, although she could think of no logical reason why that should be the case.

After lunch they returned to their fishing, and soon were

too busy to worry about weather.

For whatever reason, the ratio of black-tip sharks to other species altered dramatically during the afternoon, and they found not only hammerhead but tiger sharks as well taking the long-lines.

And once it was dark, the pace increased to reveal the best fishing they had enjoyed since the voyage began. Sharks, tuna, mackerel, all were trapped in the long runs of net that followed the *Perfidy*, and Jinx and her people were flat out keeping up with the records and tagging.

'We should have come in here in the first place,' she gasped during one welcome break about midnight. 'It's just fantastic, the variety and quantities we're taking.'

Race, who had joined the crew after dark and whose strength and experience were proving invaluable, grunted an assent that indicated that he was personally less than impressed.

'They're too close in; shouldn't be here in quantities like this,' he muttered. 'I don't begrudge you the fish, but we should have been getting results like this out around Cape Wilberforce, not here in these sheltered waters. Or up round the top of the Wessel group on our way south.'

So he was still worried about this fanciful weather change, Jinx thought, and was astonished when dawn arrived with its usual brilliant sunshine and gentle breezes. And once she'd finished breakfast, like the others she was too tired to worry about the weather. Everybody but Race flopped out either on deck or in the fo'c'sle and all were asleep within minutes.

When stirring from others wakened her near noon, Jinx opened her eyes, expecting to see some evidence of change, some logic for Race's spookiness. But the weather seemed perfectly normal, and the captain had retired to his cabin leaving Dick French in charge. The first mate showed none of Race's concern, but left no doubt in Jinx's mind when she broached the subject.

'If he's worried, there's a reason,' he declared firmly. 'I don't know how he does it, but Race Morgan has instincts most of us don't have, at least about the sea. Still, it's the wrong season for cyclones, so the most we might expect is a bloody great squall. I expect he's worried about the engine; it's been playing up since before Gove, although not seriously enough to warrant a repair job while we were there.'

Jinx was far from impressed by that particular bit of information, and immediately demanded to know more.

'Not much more to tell,' was the discouraging reply. 'The damned thing isn't exactly *wrong*, but it isn't *right* either, if you get my meaning. The kind of thing that could go on for six months and then come good with no obvious reason, or come apart in a great screaming heap this afternoon, with no warning at all.'

'But why didn't we fix it at Gove?' Jinx was truly confused now. Either the engine was healthy or it wasn't, unless of course Race was running his boat entirely on instincts. That possibility was sobering. Race Morgan didn't appear the type to bend to superstition, she thought. Or did he?

'Because there wasn't any reason to,' came the gravel-voiced reply from directly behind her. Race, as always, had approached in a predatory silence, and Jinx found herself immediately wondering how long he'd been listening.

'I'm sorry, but I really don't understand the logic of that answer,' she said, turning to find him only inches behind her, so close she was forced to look up to meet his gaze. It was unnerving.

'You should. It's the same kind of logic that has boats and ships named for women most of the time,' he told her with a half-grin that could only be described as wicked. 'That's because we're not really talking about *logic* here.

We're talking about a feeling, a suspicion that everything's not quite right. Nothing as firm or obvious as noisy tappets or screaming bearings or sticky controls. Just . . . something isn't right, that's all.'

'And so you just ignore it?' Jinx's own voice was harsh now, in response to his chauvinistic attitude and her own ignorance of things mechanical.

'Something like that.'

And now she sensed for certain that he was toying with her, deliberately seeking to stir her up. And quickly as she told herself not to, she snapped at the bait.

'You didn't ignore your *something* about the weather.'

And he grinned—a huge, pleased-with-himself, sharky grin that found no matching humour in Jinx herself.

'I can't fix the weather,' he said. 'We have to take what we get and hope for the best if my instincts are right and trouble arrives. But we can fix the engine; we've got spares for everything and all the tools.'

Jinx felt a shudder that inexplicably ran a lingering trail up her spine. And she couldn't hold back the question that followed.

'And what happens if we get both bad weather and engine trouble? Do we depend on your instincts to get us out of that?'

Race's grin remained, and Jinx found herself growing angrier by the second. He was enjoying this, and she was helping him, damn it!

'Exactly what we are doing! We're in relatively sheltered waters here, with plenty of places to run to for even better shelter. It's a helluva lot better than being out in the centre of the Gulf if things decide to go wrong. And,' he chuckled almost fiendishly, 'we're catching plenty of sharks to boot.'

Then he was gone without waiting for her reply, which was just as well, since she didn't have one that would make any sense except to a *woman's* instincts. But she was afraid, and didn't really know why.

No one else seemed bothered, and the work continued unabated until exhaustion claimed them all once more and they fell into their bunks after only a scratch meal.

Dawn came, it seemed, only moments after Jink had flopped into her hammock. And this morning it came with more than just the expected clear blue skies and gentle seas. She woke to find the skies clear enough, but the breeze was non-existent, the air was somehow heavy, difficult to breathe. And it smelled, though not with the usual thick scent of tropical flowers from the nearby land. Now the smell was turgid, thick, almost menacing in the stillness.

Jinx rolled out of the hammock and quickly made her way on deck, where Dick French and the captain were standing together and staring off to the north-east. There was no obvious concern on either man's face, but both exhibited in their posture an element of tension, a sense of waiting, watching, and awareness.

'I'm going to put the billy on. Would either of you like tea or coffee?' she asked, hesitant about breaking into their silent vigil, yet unwilling to be so rude as to ignore them by getting her own coffee without such an offer.

Both men turned as if surprised by her presence, then muttered replies and turned away just as quickly.

Jinx quickly made their coffee along with her own, and returned to the deck to find them unmoved and still silent in their watchfulness.

'What is it?' she asked, unable to contain her curiosity any longer. 'Is it the weather?'

Dick merely shrugged and took up his coffee cup. Race Morgan looked her square in the eye, but said nothing. He picked up his coffee and turned away without a word, his attention focused somewhere beyond her sight, beyond her comprehension.

Queries from the later-rising members of the crew got

no better response, except that Race gave a quick, negative
nod of his head when fishing was mentioned.

Jinx found herself waiting almost breathlessly, as much
from the tension radiating around the captain and first mate
as from the thick, sultry air. What on earth was going on?
she wondered.

But when Race finally spoke, it was only to his first mate,
and in a voice so soft it hardly carried to the others at first.

'There's a small bay just about half an hour away, good
anchorage, well sheltered,' he mused.

'Will it be right for the wind?' Dick French's voice was
equally soft, equally toned by tension.

Race shrugged, then flashed white, even teeth in a grin
that seemed to sneer at the atmosphere which now
surrounded the boat.

'If *I* am,' he replied, and turned away to take the wheel as
Dick hurried through the final check-up before starting the
engine.

Jinx could hear none of the problems both men had
discussed earlier. To her untried ear the engine sounded
smooth and operational as normal. But she needed no
experience to feel the tension that hovered like a cloud over
the boat and those responsible for it.

Even, she realised, the least experienced person aboard
couldn't miss the sultriness of the air, the thick, somehow
ominous stillness.

Before the final breakfast was completed and the washing
up done, they were anchored in a tiny lagoon and Dick was
using the dinghy to carry out a stern anchor for additional
security.

But still the sky held blue and cloudless and there seemed
no real logic to the precautions. Only instinct!

'What a perfect spot!'

Vivian Doherty's voice seemed to cut through the tension.
She was last on deck, her mane of auburn hair flying in

her habitual ponytail and her magnificent body scarcely concealed by the ragged bikini that was her habitual working gear.

To be fair, Jinx's own working attire was hardly less revealing, but she often found herself making unfair comparisons. Perhaps, she thought, it was the sheer, Junoesque proportions of the other girl. At any rate, she never felt that her own slender figure was even half so much on display.

'I love it,' Vivian continued. 'And if we're not going to fish, I reckon a swim wouldn't go amiss. Who's going to stand shark guard?'

'Nobody. And nobody's going swimming either.'

Race's voice was soft, yet somehow harsh with the conviction of his authority. Even Vivian didn't voice any objection; she merely threw him a curious glance.

One dark eyebrow slowly lifted, holding her eyes as he turned slightly and peered down through the crystal waters. Both Vivian and Jinx followed his gaze.

Both girls gasped, and Vivian was the first to speak.

'Right on, skipper,' she said, turning away to where Dick French was returning in the dinghy. 'You'd best get yourself aboard, Dick,' she called. 'Skipper's parked us fair in the middle of things this time!'

An understatement if ever there was one, Jinx thought, her own gaze still locked on the prehistoric, evil shape of the gigantic crocodile that was slowly cruising from beneath the boat.

It was, luckily, headed in the opposite direction from where Dick was rowing slowly back to the boat, but she couldn't help wondering where it had been when he'd started out. Had it been attracted by the splash of the main anchor, the lowering of the small dinghy, or perhaps Dick's splash in tossing the stern anchor into the sea?

'It isn't quite as big as it looks.'

'It wouldn't have to be,' she replied to Race's soft-spoken comment. 'Even half as big is too damned big for me, thank you.'

True enough! The reptile, now almost beyond sight, had been the dangerous side of five metres in length, even considering refraction. Longer than the dinghy!

'Don't let him bother you. Nobody's going to be swimming, or even fishing, in this little bay,' said Race. And he looked again towards the horizon.

Jinx thought for an instant that his eyes lost focus, that his nostrils flared liked those of some wild thing, scenting and seeing beyond her merely mortal facility. It was uncanny.

Dick was back aboard, and the dinghy hauled to its normal place on the top deck. Race's attention was no longer on the fierce reptilian predator. It couldn't harm the boat, she thought, and yet how could Race so easily ignore its presence?

Once again she looked in the direction where Race's attention had focused, and for an instant she didn't believe her own eyes. Far off, on the fringes of the horizon, beyond the green and lush vegetation on the islands and headlands, the sky was disappearing!

A rain squall? A cyclone? No, she decided immediately, a cyclone it just couldn't be, not at this time of year. But some weather phenomenon, something Race Morgan had sensed with primitive or supersensitive perception, something expected, something potentially dangerous.

'Batten everything down, children. It mightn't be much, but on the other hand it could be a helluva blow.'

Everyone's attention now was on the incoming weather pattern, and Dick French's commands needed no shouted urgency to get a response. Jinx wondered if everyone aboard had been able to sense the dangers so obvious to their captain. They stowed everything loose, tied down the dinghy and closed up the fo'c'sle, but all hands stayed on deck to watch the astonishing approach of what now was clearly a rain squall of immense proportions.

Race stalked from his cabin to the deck, his bare feet gripping the decking, his eyes locked on the dark of the approaching storm.

'Not a word on the radio from anywhere,' he growled in response to an unasked question from the first mate. 'I reckon it came out of nowhere and it'll end up the same place.'

Then he grinned that fierce, challenging grin Jinx had come to expect, and said, 'Pity we had to be in its way, though. Could be a helluva blow before it's over.'

He laughed, then. She didn't see the humour in it.

Everyone's attention now was fixed to the disappearing horizon, especially that of the captain. The darkness moved with deceptive speed, catching up the sun, darkening the day almost to the intensity of a tropical night as the cloud mass scudded closer.

And now the water, too, showed the approaching storm. Frist in a series of tiny, almost delicate wave patterns that flicked across the surface of the small bay, moving first towards the boat from the east, then turning upon themselves and strengthening, then turning yet again and strengthening even more.

The enormous Tiny looked increasingly nervous, as did the first mate. Only Race seemed to hold his attitude of strength; indeed, he seemed to revel in the approach of the storm, growing in stature himself as their world diminished beneath the darkening sky.

When the first of the rain arrived, tentatively and then with an almost animal roar, he bared his teeth and straightened to meet the soaking wind, then ordered everyone not of the boat's proper crew to get below and keep out of the way. The order brooked no opposition, not even from Jinx.

'It's likely to get a lot worse,' he growled as he took her by the arm and steered her after the others. 'We know what we're about, don't worry about that.'

'I'm not worried,' she protested, shouting now against the force of the wind. 'But . . .'

'But nothing! We may have trouble, and I don't want your mob getting in the way, so get out of it,' he snapped. 'Besides, this rain's doing nothing for your hairdo.'

And his grin faded as he thrust her through the hatchway to the fo'c'sle, both of them stumbling as the boat gave a sudden lurch. The hatchway slammed behind her, but not before the boat gave another violent roll and she heard Dick French's voice rise in concern. The words were lost in the deluge of rain and wind, but she heard—or thought she did—the word 'Anchor!'

The next few minutes, or perhaps it was longer, everyone spent trying to hang on to anything solid, anything that would keep them from being flung violently about in the confined space of the fo'c'sle. The boat leaped, seemed to spin like a bucking horse, first the bow and then the stern heaving, twisting.

Jinx felt sick; Brian Roberts *was* sick, and even Vivian looked the worse for the frantic, unpredictable movement of the boat. Inside the fo'c'sle, day had turned to night as waves crashed around them and the boat rocked and heaved against the anchor lines.

Then the hatch smalled open to admit the rain-soaked figure of Race Morgan, his jaw set in stern lines and his eyes smoky with determination. He said nothing, but began scrabbling in the storage locker, tossing scuba gear out behind him.

Air tanks, mask, flippers . . . the wetsuit he jammed back into the locker with a muttered oath about not enough time, then turned to Jinx with urgency in his glance.

'Get me into this,' he demanded, muscled hands thrusting

the double air tank at her, and turning his back so she could slip the harness over his shoulders.

'But . . . you can't go down in this!' she protested, the words emerging unbidden as she realised with horror what he intended.

'If I don't, we may all go down,' he gritted. 'The main anchor's dragging something awful and there's no other way. Now hurry, damn it!'

Jinx obeyed him, reaching to get the harness into place and then stooping quickly to hand him the face-mask and flippers. But when he stalked through the hatchway she was right behind him, one hand out to help steady herself against the rolling motion of the boat.

On deck, it was clear the dragging anchor was indeed a danger. The bow was turning sideways to the waves; already water was spewing across the deck, although so fierce was the downpour from above it was difficult to tell which water came from waves and which from rain.

Race was in no doubt, however.

'Tiny! We'll need your strength to guide the winch once I'm down there,' he called, kneeling to snug on the broad rubber swimming fins that would give him extra swimming power under water. 'You'll have to keep giving me slack so I can find a decent place to jam the anchor, then bring her back into line slowly and steadily. I don't think we'll get more than one chance, so be careful.'

Careful! Jinx had a horrifying mental vision of the enormous crocodile they'd seen earlier, then another of the vast number of sharks, including too many hammerheads and tiger sharks not so very far away.

Stumbling against the combined rain and wind, her feet steady enough but the rest of her being hammered first from one side and then the other, she found her way to where Morgan was braced against the rail, the swimming mask in his hands.

'Isn't there another way?' she cried, her voice whipping away in the wind gusts, her mouth filling with water as she opened it, her eyes stung by the fiercely blown droplets.

'What the hell are you doing out here? Get back inside the fo'c'sle!'

'While you do your best to get yourself killed? There must be something useful I can do,' she cried.

'There is. Use your head as something to think with and get the hell back under cover.' Race's voice was brusque, but in his eyes there was something . . . some feeling, some emotion she couldn't quite interpret.

'But . . . the crocodile . . . the sharks?'

His reply was a grin, teeth flashing against the darkness of his skin, against a sudden flare of lightning from the sky behind them. And with the lightning, thunder that struck like cannon-fire from hell.

Jinx flinched at the assault, but Race's grin didn't even falter. He reached out briefly, his fingers just brushing her cheek as he spoke.

The wind stole his words; the thunder boomed over them. And she watched in horror, then, as he did a neat backward roll over the rail and plunged into the frothing water with his hands clasped to hold the mask in place.

For an instant she saw his shape twist away, then it was lost in the frothing of the waters and she turned away to rush to the bow, where Tiny crouched by the anchor winch, his huge form cowering beneath the elemental assault of wind and rain and waves. One huge hand gripped gently at the slackened cable, the other gripped the winch handle in a grasp so tight it seemed he could bend the metal.

Jinx braced herself beside him, her own grasp two-handed along the rail as she tried to peer beneath the storm-tossed water, tried to follow the anchor-line's tortured path through the waves. Impossible.

Where only hours—or was it only minutes?—before, the

water had been glass-clear, the bottom seemingly only inches away, now all was froth and wave-driven sand.

As she watched, Tiny's enormous hands began to ease off the winch, the man governing his actions by touch alone, handling the heavy chain as if it was the lightest of fishing line and obviously in invisible touch with his captain below. Jinx could see the line moving now, inching its way outwards as Tiny fed out increasing slack. But as the chain moved, so did the boat, still lurching and bucking in the combined frenzy of wind and surf and rain. Increasingly, the boat seemed to turn broadside to the waves; and increasingly it seemed as if the storm must throw them over sideways or twist the stern anchor also free from the bottom.

Then there was a shift in the wind, a curious whirlpool effect being created in the waters dead ahead, lightening the swirls of sand and sea so that she could see—if only for an instant—the white T-shirt beneath the gleaming air tanks, his body moving in exaggerated slow motion as Race strained to carry the heavy anchor forward. Then the storm swirled away her vision, and she could see only the spume and wind-tossed waves.

A few minutes later it was all over. Without warning, the sleek, bronzed figure of Race Morgan surfaced beside the boat, and with Dick French's help clambered aboard.

'I might have to go back down when it's time to free the anchor,' gasped Race after he'd been relieved of tanks and mask, 'but that's something we can worry about when the time comes.'

Without pausing for breath, he went forward to help Tiny with the winch, but even two such powerful men couldn't force the boat around against the malicious wind and waves.

'We'll have to use the engine; there's no alternative,' Race decided aloud. 'But gently, Dick, because I've got a feeling this is when it's all going to come apart.'

'Just water in your ears,' the first mate replied, but

his grin was as phoney as his assurance. And rightly so.

Jinx felt the engine start up, felt the boat begin to forge ahead as the mighty winch took up the slack in the anchor cable. She watched as the boat slowly turned bow to the wind, slowly began to move forward until both anchor chains were taut and firm. And she heard the sudden clatter, then silence, as the engine blew.

CHAPTER SEVEN

'YOU were right, Jinx. We should have done this back at Gove.'

Race grinned wearily at her from across a deck strewn with dismantled engine components. His face, like everyone else's, was a study of grease and oil smudges and lines of fatigue.

Two days they'd been at it, everyone involved in one way or another as the massive engine was hoisted up on deck and reduced to a welter of greasy, oily bits and pieces that all had to be spotless before repairs could be completed.

Dick French had, luckily, shut down before the disintegrating bearing had caused other damage, but that did nothing to ease the repair burden. Every single part of the filthy engine had to be checked and double-checked. It was dirty, fiddly and exhausting work, improved not at all by the incessant rocking of the still-anchored boat and the lack of proper facilities, but nobody yet had dared to complain.

It was, Jinx thought, a small enough price to pay for having survived the storm. And they might not have managed that if the old engine hadn't held up long enough to get the anchors properly secured.

Her own puny gasp of apprehension at the breakdown had been swallowed by the wind, but Race Morgan's howl of anger and defiance had challenged even the storm. Her mind still held a picture of him lunging forward to lock the winch, leaping with predatory speed and balance and ignoring the risks on the slippery, wind-blown deck.

Once satisfied the anchor was set, he had turned and

126

thrust a thumbs-up signal to the dismayed first mate in the wheelhouse, then stood glaring into the wind, as if daring the storm to do its worst. And on the deck he had stayed, seemingly impervious to the wind and rain, elemental in his defence of the ship, in his defiance of the storm. He was there an hour before it became clear the danger was past.

In crisis, he had been almost frighteningly efficient, his every move a study in balance and power. Now, his face smudged with engine grease and his head sagging with the weariness they all shared, he had the engaging look of a small boy at play.

'At least in Gove we could have managed to swim.' Vivian's voice chopped through Jinx's introspection, the comment drawing an immediate reply from the first mate.

'You can go for a swim here, if you're game enough. But I wouldn't advise it. That old croc knows we're here, and I'd bet next week's wages he's just waiting for somebody as tasty as you.'

Vivian laughed, the sound tinkling in the warm sunlight. 'If you hadn't broken the engine, we'd have been able to catch him a shark to play with, and then we could swim in peace,' she jibed.

'If the engine hadn't broken itself,' Dick replied solemnly, 'we could be catching *you* a shark to play with, and you'd be too busy working to worry about having a swim.'

'At least I'd be clean.' Vivian looked with disgust at her oil-stained fingers.

The verbal sniping had been going on since they'd begun work on the engine, and the harmless badinage seemed to Jinx a healthy way of blowing off steam.

Race's people, she knew, had never doubted his ability to get them through the storm. Of her own crew she was less sure, although shed doubted seriously that a mere storm could frighten Vivian. The redhead, now settled into the team and having long ago shed Morgan's 'show pony' image, was becoming a firm friend and co-worker, despite a truly astonishing ability to find trouble.

Jinx herself, surprisingly enough, had experienced no fear at all during the storm, except for Race Morgan and the risks he'd taken. She too had found herself totally confident in him during the crisis.

They finished the engine early that afternoon, and by dark it was reinstalled and running happily. Everybody cheered, Race declared the effort deserved a tot of rum for all hands, then astonished everyone by declaring further that the next day would be a holiday.

'And what's more, I can promise you absolutely top swimming in the bargain,' he said. 'Not entirely risk-free, but in *fresh* water.'

This brought a chorus of cheers, with Vivian's voice quite the loudest. But Jinx, too, was pleased by the concept of a proper swim, although she found herself wondering why Race had looked at her so speculatively before making the suggestion.

Everyone was thoroughly tired out by their labours with the engine, and the tropical night was barely upon them before the celebration broke up. Jinx was asleep almost immediately, only to be wakened within minutes, it seemed, but the muted roar of the engine starting.

Puzzled, she slipped into her clothes and emerged on deck, to find the boat moving slowly through a night sprinkled with stars and the brightest moon she'd seen in years. The wake of the boat was strewn with incandescence like a rainbow across black velvet, and ahead the sea was mirror-still.

There was no lights in the wheelhouse, but Race's cocky grin was reflected in the moonlight as he acknowledged her presence with a gesture indicating that she should make coffee for them both. Jinx waved her agreement and joined him five minutes later with the steaming cups on a tray from the galley.

'Splendid,' he said. 'How did you know I'd be dying for a cuppa about this time?'

'Oh, I just thought there must be some logical reason for being wakened from a sound sleep that was supposed to end in a day's holiday,' she responded tartly. 'Where in heaven's name are you going in the middle of the night?'

His grin was infectious. 'To where you can have your holiday, of course. No sense waiting until morning; we'd have lost half the day getting there. This way everybody will be rested up and raring to go by the time we arrive.'

'Everybody but you,' scowled Jinx. 'And I think you needed the rest most of all. You've hardly stopped since the storm.'

'I'm OK. And you must have got enough sleep or the boat starting up wouldn't have wakened you this thoroughly,' he said. 'Glad it did, though. This coffee really hits the spot.'

He leaned back, one hand toying with the wheel as he sipped at the coffee, his attention divided between Jinx and the water ahead.

'You're welcome, I suppose,' said Jinx. 'And you're probably right about the sleep too. I just died.'

'Not surprising,' he grinned. 'The last couple of days have been pretty tough on everybody. It's going to cost me a packet in bonuses when we get back to Darwin, especially for your mob.'

'My mob? But you're not responsible for paying my people anything,' she protested, eyes wide with confusion. She suddenly had that feeling of being manipulated, and her defences needed gathering, she felt.

'I'm responsible for turning the whole lot into motor mechanics,' Race replied grimly. 'And that wasn't part of the arrangement at all. I don't expect a swimming holiday will be quite enough to square things away.'

'In fresh water? After a week at sea? I think you underestimate the allure,' laughed Jinx. 'Vivian would kill for it. And so would I, or just about,' she added, glancing down at where grease stains were still faintly visible on hands and thighs.

'I'll have to remember that,' Race said, a curious half-grin twisting his mobile mouth. 'Handy to know, a thing like that.'

Jinx didn't reply. She met his eyes silently, only too aware of how small the wheelhouse was, how near *he* was! He had only to reach out, she realised, had only to touch her and all defence would be gone. The wheelhouse had become a trap, now, charged with Race's vitality, alive with all the implied sexuality of a boudoir.

He lazed casually, his fingers caressing the wheel and his eyes caressing Jinx openly, deliberately. His gaze ran from her sleep-tousled hair down along a body over which a T-shirt and shorts suddenly seemed totally inadequate covering. It was slow, sensual and commanding, that gaze. Race's ice-green eyes seemed to physically touch her, to linger across the slim line of her throat, to brush lightly against her breasts, lifting the nipples to arousal. Jinx found her breath shortening, found herself responding, almost swaying towards him, mesmerised.

When he finally reached out to her, having dared to risk breaking the spell by putting down his coffee-cup, by stealing a seaman's quick glance at the sea ahead, she found herself unable, unwilling, to resist. His fingers closed lightly around one wrist and he drew her inexorably towards him without a word, without any real pressure except that of his will.

His lips against hers were silken-soft, gentle as the swell of the night sea. One huge hand curved around the small of her back, drawing her against him, but doing so with total awareness of her own responses. She knew that any rejection, any move on her part demanding release would be met without objection. Not that there was any need; she was more than content to be held, to meet his kisses with a slowly rising passion she couldn't deny.

His hands caressed her; his body was warm against her own, vibrant, and totally masculine. Like her, he wore only shorts and a T-shirt, and they might both have been naked for all the barrier the flimsy clothing provided.

Jinx's nipples were erect, her breasts crushing against him, and she could feel his manhood firm against her, feel a desire that matched the one growing like wildfire inside her. Her arms clasped around his neck, her fingers tangling in the crisp curls at his nape as she met his embrace. The rush of blood inside her drowned the faint clatter of the engine; her eyes closed in ecstasy as his fingers trailed along her spine, across her shoulderblades.

It was madness, she knew. Madness spurred by her memories of the storm, by the black velvet night around them, by fantasies unrealised within her.

Madness, but she no longer cared. She could have fought him, probably would have at another time and place, but now there was no fight, no need for fighting between them.

'Today . . . later . . . will be ours alone,' she heard him whisper, his breath warm against her ear. 'I have a place to show you, a magic place.'

She didn't reply, didn't need to. Instead she twisted to meet his beckoning lips, her body moving to meet his touch. When his fingers slid beneath her T-shirt, lifting to her breasts, she sighed at the tenderness of his touch. Whn his lips left her own, she moaned, then moaned even more as they cruised down to rest where his fingers had prepared the way.

And then, too soon, he eased apart the bond that had formed between them. His lips drew away, his hands gently steadied her as he ended the embrace, as reality claimed them. One hand reached to the wheel, his eyes turned to the sea and the first hints of dawn.

'Right time; wrong place,' he said, voice as velvet as the

soft-breaking on the beach ahead. 'Damn it! Nobody should
be expected to try and drive a boat and make love at the
same time.'

Jinx had no reply. His voice was still vibrant with fierce
emotion, but she knew her own would be shaking,
tremulous. The fire inside her still raged. She wanted his
kisses, his touch. But the moment of magic was ended, and
she suddenly wondered just how foolish she might have
been.

'I . . . I . . .' The sound wasn't words, just a repetitive
noise that clotted in her throat, and her eyes began to fill
with unwanted tears as she looked up into Race's face. Then
it was too much—far, far too much—and she turned and
fled from the wheelhouse, unable to cope with the mixed
emotions she now felt.

She heard his hiss of exasperation as she fled to the deck,
then slipped through the hatchway to the fo'c'sle and the
relative security of her bunk. He didn't follow. Of course he
wouldn't, she thought. And none of the other occupants so
much as stirred at her arrival.

Minutes later she heard the rattle of the anchor chain.
Wherever they were, they'd arrived.

Jinx remained abed until the rest of the crew rolled
sleepily from their bunks, but she didn't sleep, couldn't
possibly still her emotions enough, much less still the magic
memories, the fevered responses that seemed to continue
into the dawn.

As she writhed in the bunk, too warm beneath the flimsy
sheet, it seemed her body was on fire, that she would explode
into real flames. There was the same tingling sensation that
could come from severe sunburn, the same tenderness.

Her lips felt bruised, swollen from Race's kisses, and yet
she knew he had been nothing but gentle, nothing but tender
with her. Where he had kissed her, touched her, the gesture
had been totally caressing. He had held back his strength,

given her total freedom to respond in her own way, at her own pace.

And that, she found herself thinking, had been little short of wanton. Never had any man stirred her to such intimacies, to such a searing, raging sense of need!

And he'd known it—had deliberately left her with that need, had prepared her, sensitised her to his touch, to her own needs, her own desires.

When she finally emerged on deck for the second time that morning, Jinx moved shyly, self-consciously. It seemed to her that everyone on the boat must know . . . must be able to read in her eyes the feelings Race had aroused. The fact that nobody appeared to notice anything made it no easier.

Race looked up with a welcoming smile when she finally crept into the galley where most of the crew were finishing breakfast, but even in his glance there was no challenge, no smirk of victory. Jinx smiled back, but had to force the smile just a little.

Once everyone had been fed, Race announced that they would all go ashore together in the dinghy. It would be slightly overloaded, he said, but the distance was very short indeed and the tiny lagoon calm as glass.

With his comment, Jinx really looked around her, and for the first time she realised what a splendid place he had brought them to for their holiday. The lagoon with its gleaming white sands spilled down from a tall escarpment that appeared to be formed of some rich, dark stone. At least three creeks that she could see filtered down to weave a path through the sands.

Race took the shark rifle, 'just in case', and led the way along a small dune ridge to where a brilliant lake of clear fresh water was held back from the sea by a dyke in the black cap-rock.

'There'll be no sharks here, and probably no crocs either,' he said, handing over the rifle to Dick French. 'I think the water's too clear to attract the crocs, but make sure you keep a good eye out anyway.'

Both men scouted the tiny lake thoroughly before allowing the assembled crew to rush into the cool, incredibly clear water like so many children at a picnic.

They'd brought all the fixings for a barbecue lunch, and the weather was perfect for a day ashore. After a week on salt water, the very texture of the fresh, clean spring water on their grimy flesh was delightful.

Race took his first mate aside for a brief conference, then turned and gestured for Jinx to come and join him. He was already moving along the edge of the escarpment when she caught up.

'Reckon you can keep a secret?' he hissed quietly as she stepped in beside him.

She paused suspiciously.

'You're scheming again, aren't you?' she said, stretching out her stride to keep up with him. 'What kind of secret are you talking about?'

'Why is it that you never want to trust me?' he countered. 'Didn't I promise you earlier today that there would be something special, something just for us?'

Jinx paused again, certain she must be blushing violently and less than certain of what reply she dared make. Was this no more than a confirmation of an assignation?

Race grinned at her uncertainty. 'It isn't what you might be thinking,' he chuckled. 'But it definitely does involve secrets, and you have to promise you'll never reveal what I'm going to show you . . . not to anyone, even on the boat.'

'But . . . but why, for goodness' sake? What have you got back there, some pirate's treasure or something?' It wouldn't, she decided, surprise her one bit if he had.

His grin was deliberately wicked. 'Better than that; much, much better. At least it always has been for me, and I'm curious to see how you'll react.'

Suspicion continued. 'Is this some kind of test?'

'Not really.'

They were well out of sight of the others now, moving along the largest of the creeks through sprinkled groves of pandanus and paperbarks. Ahead, Jinx could see that the black cap-rock seemed to have been formed on sandstone, or perhaps limestone, and the effects of erosion were quite spectacular.

Race was watchful now. There would always be the risk of snakes, and both of them wore only light sneakers. Jinx gradually fell in behind him, and travelled single file effectively defeated the ability to communicate while on the move.

Once he paused, apparently to re-check his bearings, then turned away from the main creek on to a branch that seemed to pour directly from the walls ahead. As they approached, it became obvious that the creek had carved a narrow gorge through the soft stone, and Race paused with a smile at the entrance.

'From here on, it gets more and more interesting,' he said. 'We should be able to right through to the centre of the island, unless something's happened to the caverns. I presume you're not afraid of bats?'

Jinx suppressed a shudder. She wasn't exactly *afraid* of bats, but they were far from being her favourite creatures.

'Does that mean we're going into bat caves?' she asked, expecting the answer but wanting more detail before she committed herself.

'Sort of. More of a tunnel than a cave, though. And from the looks of the creek level we may have to swim for it in places, or at least wade through some pretty deep holes. And there's bound to be a few bats, although if we don't need torches we shouldn't disturb them much.'

'And what about crocs? Or snakes?'

'No worries at all, except maybe for the snakes. I'll go

first anyway, if that's any consolation,' he replied with his usual cocky grin. 'Even carry you, if the water gets too deep.'

'I'm quite capable of swimming, and you know it,' Jinx replied sternly. Race was up to something, but she was damned if she'd now give him the satisfaction of playing great white hero as well.

'Right. Let's get started, then, or we'll end up missing lunch,' he said, and plunged into the first of a series of pools leading into the rock.

Centuries of erosion from the sandstone had given the creek a smooth, sandy bottom, and they moved quickly through a series of pools and channels that gradually became darker and darker. Yet ahead was always enough light to navigate by, and periodically they passed under narrow fissures where the cap-rock was incomplete and light spilled down in fanciful patterns.

Twice they had to swim, once for nearly fifty metres with the carvern roof close above their heads and the sound of disturbed bats swishing backwards and forwards in the darkness.

'You OK?' asked Race, and despite an intense desire to be almost anywhere else, Jinx grunted in the affirmative.

And when they finally emerged into normal light, she gasped at the sheer majesty of the scene. Their grotto now became a large, hanging valley, surrounded by the sandstone walls, but with an environment all its own. The pool at the centre was cooler even than the creek they'd travelled, and the rugged sandstone had been carved into battlements, caves and overhangs. It was like something from science fiction.

'It's unbelievable!' Jinx cried, looking round in pure and honest delight. 'Like a whole hidden world where nobody's ever been before.'

She followed Race to the far side of the valley, where a vast outthrust of rock had created an enormous sheltered

area, and immediately realised her mistake. It was
immediately clear that many people had been there before.
The floor of the overhang was thick with charcoal from
centuries of cooking fires, and as Jinx stooped to follow
Race's lead beneath the ledge, she could only gasp in
astonishment.

The entrance was deceptive, and what appeared to be
only an overhang now revealed the start of a vast cave
network that stretched back through a series of caverns
beneath the cap-rock. And on the walls were some of the
most incredible Aboriginal artworks. Jinx had seen a variety
in her travels, but nothing of this quality, nothing of this
magnitude. Entire walls flowed with patterns of dugongs,
fish and native animals in red ochre, some yellow material
and charcoal blacks.

'It's . . . it's just overwhelming!' she cried, reaching out to
Race, tugging at his arm to slow his progress. And overwhelming, she immediately decided, was an understatement.

These paintings were old! Primitive, and so intense they
could make the hair prickle at the nape of her neck. Such
clarity, such astonishing attention to detail!

On one side, a dugong swam in perfect balance and
symmetry, while further along a shark clearly identifiable as
a tiger-shark glided along a rock seam as if alive.

As they moved further into the complex, the paintings
differed. Now there were hands—hundreds of hands and all
individually unique—patterned on the roof like some
primaeval wallpaper. They had been painted in the
Aboriginal method of blowing red ochre across the artist's
own hand, and Jinx marvelled at the effect.

'How did they get up there?' she asked, voice low in a
whisper because it seemed almost sacrilegious to speak aloud
in this place. 'The ceiling's forty feet up in places.'

Race shrugged. 'Maybe some kind of scaffolding, or
maybe the floor's eroded that much since then.'

His voice, too, was held deliberately low, almost a feline purr in the hushed atmosphere. Both of them realised the incredible age of the paintings, or at least of most. There were a few, on just one wall of one cavern, that were clearly more modern. They depicted, in startling detail, visitors of Asian features and ships that were classically both Asian and European in type. And here too, for the first time, there was artistic evidence of the culture clashes that had followed. A stick figure cast a long war spear; another held what could only be some type of firearm.

As they moved into yet another cavern, Jinx found herself clutching Race Morgan's arm, and both of them moving with exaggerated caution through the cave system.

'I shouldn't be here,' she found herself whispering, voice so soft he couldn't possibly hear. And she realised that indeed she shouldn't be here. These were sacred sites without question, and when they turned the next corner she cried out softly in alarm.

'Damn! I'd forgotten about this part,' Race cursed beneath his breath. He half turned to shield her from the paintings, but it was already too late.

What had so startled Jinx was a life-sized portrait that seemed ready to leap from high on the wall, and as she looked up it was to see another, equally graphic, etched on the low ceiling of the cavern. Both were clearly Aboriginal, almost certainly very, very ancient, and both were graphically, exaggeratedly male. They clutched themselves with one hand, their fighting spears with the other, and there was a definite element of some ancient, alien magic about them.

This cave, Jinx knew instinctively, was not for women's eyes. Not the eyes of Aboriginal women past or present, and not for her eyes either. She shuddered at the atmosphere of this final cavern and was turning away even as Race cursed.

Once free of the cavern system, she found it difficult to credit the feelings she had had, feelings of breaking some taboo she could never understand, of somehow intruding into something that still held ominous vibes.

It was so easy to let imagination go wild, here, to visualise the naked black warriors who would have used such an initiation cave, to hear the eerie, haunting moans of their didgeridoos, the rattling of spears.

Jinx had occasionally enjoyed the rhythmic sound of a didgeridoo played in an authentic Aboriginal ceremony, but that had been in a modern setting, in more or less modern circumstances. There was nothing modern about this hidden valley, nothing modern about the startlingly artistic creations of the caverns. This was ancient Australia and would remain so.

'How did you ever find this place?' she found herself asking Race, her voice still hushed in reverence for her surroundings.

'I grew up with some of the few remaining people whose sacred place this is,' he replied. 'Virtually none of them left now. I shouldn't have taken you into that last cave, even so. I'd honestly forgotten how malignant it can appear.'

'You shouldn't have brought me at all, should you?'

'How else could you see it? And I mean more than just see. A place like this isn't something you just look at; you have to experience it. But you can understand why I wanted your promise of secrecy.' He smiled. 'And it must be obvious I know you're not a souvenir hunter or a vandal, or you certainly wouldn't be here.'

'I should certainly think so,' Jinx replied. 'I suppose that's one reason you came in the night, is it?'

'And will go in the darkness, after everybody's asleep tonight,' he said. 'Actually, I imagine the crew could probably find the place again if they thought it was important enough, but since none of them has seen this place, I wouldn't expect problems. And Tiny, of course, wouldn't be caught dead within five miles of here. If he knew this place existed, I doubt if you'd get him on to the island at all.'

'But he's not from this region, surely?' Jinx was dredging her memory, sifting through scraps of information picked up over the years. Not enough.

'No, he's from somewhere near Broome, originally, and of course he's of mixed blood. But he's still strongly tribal in some respects, and he'd think this place was just too strong in magic; best avoided at all cost.'

'You don't seem worried by that.' It wasn't exactly a question, but her way of making the statement begged an answer, and Race didn't disappoint.

'I don't believe in this kind of magic, exactly,' he told her with conviction.

They were sprawled comfortably in the sand at the edge of the pool, their legs cool in the water and their clothing gradually drying in the intense tropical sun. Jinx found herself wanting to draw Race out, to somehow learn to understand him better. When they had started out that morning, considering their encounter in the wheelhouse, she had been almost positive his real motivation was quite different from what it had turned out. Now she wasn't sure at all.

He had made no move since leaving the others to pick up where they had left off, and Jinx found it mildly confusing to be unsure if that was what she wanted or not.

Watching him, seeing the rippling play of muscles, the vital masculinity and that haunting sense of the predator, she found his gentleness of the night before intriguing, as was today's role as guide, of secret-sharer.'

'You've never brought anyone here before, have you?' she asked, and knew the answer even before he nodded agreement. The response sent a thrill surging through her. This was something special between them, truly a secret shared.

'Thank you,' she said simply. 'It's so truly beautiful here, almost magical. I'm very glad you brought me.'

'Even if I don't believe in the magic?'

He was teasing now, and the grin and expression in those pale green eyes made it obvious.

'The magic is here, whether you believe in it or not,' Jinx retorted with a smile of her own. 'And if you expect me to believe you're too insensitive to recognise it, then you'd best think again.'

'Oh, the magic's here . . . for sure. And I'm not rubbishing it, not at all. You couldn't possibly go through those caverns, view those incredible works of art, and then start rubbishing the magic.'

He was suddenly more serious than his earlier tone had indicated, and Jinx listened with growing interest as he related boyhood experiences with the Aboriginals. It wasn't that he didn't believe in their magic, he eventually explained, but that their magic was 'different' for them, and so too was the way of believing.

'But a place like this, I agree, has something uniquely magic, something any person should be able to feel. The trouble with so many of the more accessible sacred sites and Aboriginal art galleries is the number of yobbo types that vandalise and ruin them,' he said.

'It's the same everywhere, not just places like this,' Jinx replied, sympathising with his view and sharing his general concern.

'True, but sometimes I think it's worse when natural monuments are destroyed or vandalised, because the historic significance is so very great. Look at this place! The original people who created it are gone, their descendants are scattered and have virtually lost their culture, and there simply is nobody left who could even properly interpret these paintings.'

Race was on his feet now, striding back and forth along

the minuscule beach, clearly concerned with his own responsibilities in the matter.

'And what am I supposed to do? You're pleased to have seen them, but not entirely convinced of your right to see them. I'm not even sure *I* have any right to the knowledge of this place, but if I haven't—if *we* haven't—then perhaps nobody will ever again.

'I've tried to visit every year for . . . oh, more than twenty years now. And never once have I seen a single sign that anybody but me has been here in all that time. Nobody since I was shown the place as a child. Only me.'

'Perhaps others come who care as much as you do, who try to make certain they don't leave signs of their passing,' Jinx suggested. 'Surely all the people to whom this place is important can't be gone.'

'There were very few of the old ones left even when I was a boy,' he explained soberly. 'My father used to fish up this way, and do a bit of croc shooting back when it was legal. He knew some of the old-timers then, which of course is how I know about this place. But I haven't met a proper tribal Aborigine from this place *anywhere* since I grew up and started fishing myself.'

They talked for a few minutes more, then at Race's suggestion began the lengthy trek back to the beach and their companions.

'If we're gone too long, we'll miss lunch, and apart from the fact that I need it, there's no logic in causing idle talk,' he said.

Jinx found this change from rough and ready seaman to protective philosopher a touch different to assimilate, especially as she'd been given no insight as to the reasons for his apparent change in attitude towards her. And would he change once more when they got back? she wondered.

Race Morgan did change, and it was an abrupt, shocking change, but not for any reasons Jinx might have pondered.

The transformation was instant, and it occurred just as they left the gut of the gorge, retracing their way along the creek towards the beach.

They could hear nothing of their companions yet, but both halted in surprise at the unexpected sound of a gunshot from somewhere in the direction of the beach.

Race halted, but only for an instant. 'Try and keep up,' he ordered and was away, running lightly along the soft creek bed even as the gun discharged again. He was already out of sight when the third shot boomed away the solitude of the island. And when Jinx emerged from the final bit of cover, breasting the sand ridge above the swimming pond, she found he had already reached their crew.

Everyone but her was assembled in a huddle on the beach, and they weren't alone. Gathered beside a luxurious dinghy, clearly from the even more luxurious yacht anchored in the tiny bay, were Melissa Stewart, a distinguished-looking man whom Jinx assumed to be her father, and several other men.

CHAPTER EIGHT

'THERE'S no argument and no room for argument. We're going back to Darwin. We're going straight back and we're leaving now.'

Jinx gritted her teeth, staring angrily into Race's icy eyes. She was worse than angry; she was almost speechlessly furious. Bad enough, she thought, that he wouldn't—couldn't—tell her *why* their voyage had been so abruptly called off. Worse was his unarguable insistence that Melissa would be sailing with them.

Jinx couldn't argue the first. Not without more information, which Race hadn't provided. And she didn't even dare mention the second; she would be unable to do so without blowing her stack entirely, and she knew it.

'Look,' he said sternly. 'My orders are to return immediately. No more fishing, no more research. Home!'

'But with no reason? And why would my boss issue those orders to *you*? I realise you're the captain and I don't dispute that, but this is *my* research voyage and I haven't even so much as been consulted.'

'You know as much about that as I do. My orders came through Mel Stewart, and they're obviously up to date or he wouldn't have come all this way to find us. You do realise that I saw him in Gove, and nothing was mentioned then.'

Jinx could see the writing on the wall. Race had no choice, and worse, he had no real information. Only the message brought by Mel Stewart, who Jinx thought privately was the archetypal father for a bitch like Melissa.

He was smarmy, so full of himself there wasn't room for anything else, and, worst of all, he fancied himself as

God's gift to womanhood. His attitude on being introduced
to her once she had caught up with Race at the beach had
been so oily as to be offensive, and he had hovered round
Vivian with all the subtlety of a dog in heat.

'I don't like the man and I don't trust him,' she protested.
'If there's to be a change, the orders should have come to
me, damn it. Not that you care if he treats me like some
damned virgin with the vapours!'

Race's laugh was less than friendly. His eyes glittered with
strange lights, and his voice was throaty when he replied.

'So he's a bit of a chauvinist. Most men are, up here, and
I've sure never met a politician who wasn't. Look at this
from your boss's point of view. He's probably got no other
way of getting to us, if he's a typical public servant, so he's
used the network he's used to, and since Stewart knows me
and doesn't know you, he's passed the message on that way.'

'But . . .'

'But nothing. We're going straight back and we're
stopping for nothing short of the worst weather. End of
story. Once we hit Darwin you can get on the phone and
scream your heart out, but until then . . .'

'I know. Behave myself . . . don't make waves . . . don't
cause upsets among the crew. Yes, sir. No, sir.'

Jinx spat out the final words, doing so over her shoulder
because she was already half-way out of the cabin door,
which she ceremoniously slammed behind her.

'Damn it . . . damn it . . . damn it!' she muttered as she
stormed through to the fo'c'sle where her own crew were.

'No joy with the skipper, hey? I'm not surprised,' said
Vivian on Jinx's entrance. 'And you shouldn't be either,'
she added less vehemently. 'Mel Stewart carries a lot of
weight here in the Territory; he's got heaps of power and
fingers in every pie that's going. Even without the daughter,
I'd expect a smart businessman like Morgan to at least pay
attention.'

'Pay attention? He practically sat up and begged!' Jinx made no attempt to hide her anger. She felt totally betrayed, and Melissa's involvement in the situation only rubbed salt into the wounds. Not that she would ever, ever admit that.

Straight back, the great Captain Morgan had said. Well, she thought, he'd better pray for good weather and clear sailing, because Melissa had been on the boat only hours and was already starting to create dissension.

She had snubbed Tiny in a gesture with racial overtones that had drawn a growl from Dick French. She had petulantly dismissed Vivian's preparations for the lunch on the beach, and her singular contact with Jinx had showed that the violence at Gove was very much young Melissa's style. She was a nasty piece of work at such close quarters.

Jinx waved aside further discussion, needing all her concentration just to keep from screaming. Damn Race Morgan, she thought. And double-damn to her absent boss, whom she knew to be sufficiently public-service orientated that he might never bother to tell her why she had been so presumptuously recalled.

It could be anything, and Jinx unfortunately knew that only too well. Office politics, a paper-shuffling mix-up, a casual word over coffee. It took so little to create disruption in a large organisation like hers . . . and with a boss like hers!

Women in science, she thought, might gradually be gaining more and better jobs, more and better recognition, but it was an uphill battle all the way, especially with chauvinistic, career-protecting bosses like her own.

She glanced out of the porthole, noting that Race was already making good time. They had steamed between Elcho and Drysdale Islands and were boring almost due west across the fluid expanse of the Arafura Sea.

Darwin in two days and a bit, if the weather helped and the engine held. It should, she thought, considering the amount of work her own crew had spent on it. And for what?

The rest of the day was boring—no other way to describe it. Melissa might swan aobut the confines of the boat, but Jinx had neither reason nor inclination to follow suit. Melissa might spend half her time clinging like a leech to Race Morgan's muscular arm; Jinx didn't even want to see him, much less touch him.

When she'd caught up at the beach, her first concern was that somebody else had actually found Race's secret island. That Mel Stewart and his daughter might be a threat to her own future wasn't in consideration; Race's attitude towards this island and its secrets was far more important.

Until Race had gone off down the beach with the oily politician, the two men striding far from everyone's hearing, then returning for Morgan to drop his bombshell.

'The trip's off, I'm afraid,' he had announced without preamble. 'We've been recalled to Darwin and we're to leave quick smart.'

'Not until after lunch, I hope,' Vivian had protested. 'I put a helluva lot of work into this.'

That comment had drawn Melissa's scorn, but everyone else tucked in and lunch disappeared very quickly indeed. Melissa lunched on her father's yacht.

It wasn't until they were under way that Jinx had found a moment to catch Race alone in the wheelhouse, and the argument that ensued—along with his suddenly subservient attitude to both Mel Stewart and his daughter—had quite destroyed the day for Jinx.

Melissa had come aboard with more clothes and luggage for the two or three-day run to Darwin than anyone else aboard had brought for their full month's voyage, and her immediate move into the captain's own cabin hadn't gone unnoticed.

'She does know what she wants; you've got to give her that,' somebody muttered at one point, and surprisingly enough it was Vivian who spoke in the captain's defence.

'She knows, all right, but I'll bet my severance pay she doesn't get everything as easy as it looks right now,' Vivian said. 'She's got guts, though; or else she's too dumb to realise she's playing with fire.'

Openly, of course, nobody would have dared to comment on the situation, and nothing was said in Jinx's hearing about her own relationship with Race. The fact that they'd gone off together would have been noted, but so would the sea-change since their return.

Her concern for the island's safety had got short shrift when she had finally managed to corner the captain in the wheelhouse.

'It isn't a problem,' he'd said bluntly. 'They knew roughly where we were because of radio contact with Gove while we were fixing the engine. In fact they must have been close to us yesterday, because Stewart said they just managed to keep us in sight while we steamed through the night.'

'So why didn't they use the radio?' Jinx had demanded. 'I mean, it's hardly a secret that we've been recalled, is it? Stewart knows it, his daughter knows it, his crew knows it, and I would imagine half of Nhulunbuy as well.'

'He said he presumed it was private, and since they were going this way . . .'

'To deliver our passenger?' Jinx knew she was being catty and would sound it, but she suddenly didn't care. There was something fishy going on and she found herself liking the situation less and less.

'That too, I suppose, although why she wants to get to Darwin instead of enjoying the rest of the cruise beats me. That yacht's more comfortable than the old *Perfidy*.'

Jinx could have hit him! How could a man of Race Morgan's capabilities, a man with the sensitivity she'd seen that very morning, be so taken in by a violent, scheming little bitch like Melissa?

The Stewart yacht might have been comfortable, but it

lacked the one comfort Melissa wanted most of all, and Jinx was certain the girl would have sailed on a prawn trawler if it meant sharing a cabin with Race Morgan. Although probably, she thought, not for too long. Melissa was a girl who liked her creature comforts; life on a working fishing boat, the day-to-day life of hard work, simple food and more hard work, wouldn't appeal to her at all.

Jinx had no such qualms. The speed of their return to Darwin, no matter under what cloud, would hardly give her time to complete the expedition's paperwork and sort out the various specimens that required handling.

Almost one entire freezer aboard the boat was filled with vertebrae for future examination, and tissue samples to determine freezer shrinkage, and there was a host of other samples also in need of documentation. Paperwork, Jinx often thought, would be her nemesis.

Vivian was extremely helpful. The tall redhead had decided her major contribution to the remainder of the voyage was to take over the galley.

'Somebody's got to do it,' she said. 'We both know there's somebody who *won't*, you're too busy and as far as I'm concerned none of the boys can cook anything worth a damn. We may be going back without all we set out to do, but if nothing else we're going to eat well on the way.'

And so it was. The male members of the crew were told in no uncertain terms to just do whatever work they were called upon to perform and otherwise stay out of the way. No such demands, of course, were levelled at Race or his nubile cabin-mate, but the captain's duties kept him clear of the galley except at meals, and nobody had any doubts that where he was, Melissa would be.

Between cooking chores, Vivian got stuck into helping Jinx with the mountains of paperwork that suddenly seemed to have materialised. It all worked tremendously well for the first part of the voyage.

Then, to nobody's surprise, Melissa got bored. And a bored Melissa was, also no surprise, like an overgrown, precocious, ten-year-old. Nuisance personified.

She had spent the first afternoon's travel monopolising Race Morgan to the exclusion of all else. She had clung to him like a limpet, insisted on behing allowed to drive the boat, to be shown around the vessel as if it were some tourist vessel, to have him with her while she sunbathed on the afterdeck.

'I hope she burns to a crisp,' Vivian had muttered at one point. 'With that skin, she ought to.' Her own complexion, far from what might be expected with her startling hair colour, never seemed to burn. She tanned with a rich olive tan that suited her.

It was also Vivian, predictably, who noticed that while Melissa spent that first night in the captain's cabin, she did so alone. Race, having let his first mate run the boat during daylight, took over himself once the swift-falling tropical night arrived.

Jinx wasn't interested, and tried her best to make that clear when Vivian began giving her chapter and verse the next moring.

'I don't care what either of them do,' she lied valiantly. 'All I want is to get back to Darwin so I can find out what's going on.'

But she did care! And she, also, had noticed who spent the night with whom. She had even contemplated going topside to join the captain, to try and find out more about the mystery of their being withdrawn from the expedition.

Then memory and logic had combined to kick that idea swiftly in the head. Memory of her last night with Race in the wheelhouse was sweet, poignant and self-defeating. Logic told her that if he wanted Melissa—which he obviously did—he would have her. And Jinx in the bargain, if she was stupid enough to let herself continue to be involved.

The fickleness of the man infuriated her. How could he

have made love to her only days before, taken her to a place so obviously important to him, so private and almost sacred, and then slap her down as soon as his blonde girlfriend arrived? Try as she might, Jinx couldn't rid herself of that feeling of betrayal, of having been used.

The paperwork helped, but not enough. The boat was just too small for her to avoid Race Morgan as thoroughly as she would have wished. It seemed that no matter where she looked, he was there. And usually with his blonde friend right there beside him.

And by the following morning it became immediately clear that Melissa, bored and bent on mischief, had determined her targets and was about to launch into orbit.

She started in the galley over breakfast, demanding to be served a variety of delicacies seldom available aboard the *Perfidy* and certainly not to be found this long out of port.

'But you've got freezers, and refrigerators, and all the gear,' she complained. 'So why *not* frozen orange juice? These oranges are older than Methuselah; they're not fit to make proper juice out of.'

The bacon was too fatty, the tender fillets of mackerel which Tiny had caught only hours before on a trolled handline were not to her liking, and the toast was too crisp. Only when Race, strangely silent, raised one eyebrow in warning did Melissa give over her complaints.

Her attempt to interrupt a chess game between Brian Roberts and Glen James had short shrift. They studiously ignored her until she stamped her pretty little feet and departed in a huff. And the whole crew, including Jinx, heard the result of her attempt to join Race Morgan in his cabin that morning.

At first, it was difficult to determine if the muffled sounds from the cabin indicated what Jinx most feared and loathed, but when Melissa emerged, white-faced and trembling, a few minutes later, Vivian ventured the opinion that maybe running the ship all night had put a damper on the captain's patience.

Jinx ignored the comment, just as she tried to ignore the feeling that her stomach was filled with cement and her heart with lead. She was slowly but surely tuning out, her mind seeking the only safety available. Given any choice, Race Morgan would not exist, Melissa would not exist. She would bury herself in paperwork and ignore all else.

During the morning, it worked. Vivian helped by setting herself up as defender of the galley and the need for enough privacy to tackle the paperwork. When Melissa wandered innocently in to enquire about lunch, she was handed a potato peeler and told to either work—silently—or disappear. She chose the latter.

But by afternoon, all was sweet again. At least from Melissa's point of view. The captain emerged from his cabin and straight into his role, waiting on her hand and foot, exuding charm from every pore.

Vivian declared the performance 'disgusting'. Jinx ignored it. She hadn't spoken to Race, even at mealtimes, since their last argument in the wheelhouse. And now, with her eyes aching and her entire body taut with nervous exhaustion, all she could think of was finishing the voyage, finding out what had gone wrong. And *not* thinking about Race Morgan.

She was thus almost defenceless when he came into the galley late that evening, silently poured himself coffee, and sat down across from where she was still poring over the paperwork.

'You're working too hard,' he said at last, forcing her to look up, forcing her to see him, to recognise his existence. 'Can't this wait until we get back?'

'Why?' she said angrily. 'I've nothing else to do, have I?'

'You could try taking a rest, like everybody else. You've worked hard enough on this trip to deserve it.'

'Everybody else isn't taking a rest. Vivian's been at it

since dawn and will be here again at dawn tomorrow. Your crew isn't resting. Why should I?' She refrained from mentioning that he also had been working, and was now.

'Look,' he began, 'I know this has all come as something of a shock to you, and I know it's got you upset, but . . .'

'But I should react by stretching out in the sun and just ignoring it?' Her tone was deliberately antagonistic, aided by her exhaustion in conveying an attitude of disgust. 'That's typical, I think. It's what my boss would expect, what that slimy politician mate of yours would think. And what . . .'

'And *not* what I'd think,' he interjected. 'You're not going to accomplish one damned thing by working yourself into the ground now. All you'll do is get to Darwin in a state of total exhaustion, and what'll that gain you?'

'It'll gain me just as much as sitting around here doing nothing,' snapped Jinx. 'And more than arguing with you when I could be working,' she added pointedly, returning her attention to the papers in front of her and hoping against hope that he might take the hint.

He did, after a fashion. At the very least, he shut up, although he continued to sit there, sipping at his coffee and watching her as she worked. She didn't have to look to know this; she could *feel* his eyes upon her.

The sensation was unnerving. She could feel him watching her, but even worse, could almost detect changes of his mood as he watched. There was an instant when he was distinctly angry, but another when she felt him soften. And then, in her fevered imagination, she fancied she could feel his eyes caressing her, lingering at the base of her long neck, stroking through the tangles of her hair . . .

But when she finally looked up, anger in her eyes and her expression stern, he wasn't looking at her at all. He was leaning back in his chair, eyes closed, and either deep in thought or very, very tired, she guessed.

Disturbed, she took an instant to watch him in repose, but

an image of Melissa seemed to materialise between them, and
Jinx sneered, then looked away, returning her attention to the
paperwork.

The next time she looked up, Race was gone.

She worked straight through to midnight, forcing herself
despite an admission of the exhaustion Race had so readily
seen. Then she gave it up, eyes heavy with weariness, and
after stacking the papers carefully so as to be out of Vivian's
way in the morning, she stumbled to the fo'c'sle and the
welcome of her bunk.

Dawn came, not with the sudden shaft of bright tropical
sunlight that usually woke her, but with the unexpected feel of
somebody shaking her vigorously by the shoulder and an
anxious voice urging her to wakefulness.

'. . . trouble. Come on, Jinx, get up, get up!'

She forced her eyes open, groggily shaking her head as she
stared up at Vivian, wide-eyed and clearly wide awake. And
angry!

'You're not going to believe this,' the redhead hissed,
obviously anxious not to waken anybody else in the crowded
fo'c'sle.

'Believe what?' Jinx whispered in reply, forcing her tired
body out of the bunk and reaching for her clothes. She was so-
o-o-o tired, and from the darkness it couldn't yet be sun-up.

Groggily, she allowed herself to be half dragged through on
to the deck and then into the galley, where her eyes flashed
wide with alarm and astonishment.

Everything was awash with paper. All her work, all her
hours of calculations and carefully handwritten notes were
scattered like oversized snowflakes. The entire galley looked
like the aftermath of a whirlwind.

And not only the papers. Foodstuffs, also, had been
randomly scattered. The net that held fresh vegetables had
somehow come adrift, and the floor was a litter of paper,
onions, carrots and oranges. The flour container had spilled

its contents; a bottle of tomato sauce lay half empty among the mess it had created.

Jinx felt sick. And as the two girls hastily began the messy job of trying to separate scientific data from spilled food and liquid, she felt even more sick.

'How could this happen?' she muttered. 'We didn't hit any rough weather last night, or did we?' For her own part, she couldn't be sure. Once abed, she had slept like the dead.

'Of course we bloody didn't!' was the vicious reply. 'This was deliberate, and I don't think I have to look very far to know who's responsible either.'

'What the hell!'

Race's voice was gravelly, heavy with weariness as he stood like some figure of wrath in the hatchway. He too looked appropriately stunned by the situation.

'How the hell did you manage this?' he demanded at last, and recoiled from Vivian's angry retort.

'*We* didn't, but I don't need three guesses to figure out who *did* . . . or whose bed she's sleeping in!' Vivian snarled from her crouched position half under the galley table. 'What would you call it, captain . . . vandalism, childish enthusiasm, or maybe mutiny?'

'I wouldn't call it anything without a bit more evidence than you've given me so far,' was the cold, frigid cold reply. 'I presume you're accusing Melissa, but before you go any further I'd like to know on what grounds.'

'Evidence, captain? There isn't any evidence, as you can plainly see. But you tell me who else would get anything out of creating a mess like this?' Vivian was furious, and she rose to her feet obviously prepared to make a fight of this here and now.

Jinx caught at her arm, and mentally thought herself lucky to have done so before her friend took the issue into the physical arena.

'We don't know who did this, or why,' she said firmly, trying to hide the fact that she believed exactly as Vivian, and couldn't imagine how Race could be so blind as to presume anything else himself. Nobody had reason to destroy her work; Melissa alone wouldn't need a reason.

'You may not have any proof, but I don't need any to figure this out,' snapped Vivian, twisting in a bid to free herself from Jinx's grip. 'Nobody else on the boat would have the slightest reason for this sort of thing.'

'And what makes you think Melissa would have any reason? She's got nothing to do with this research programme.' Race stayed firm in his defence of the young blonde, but Vivian's anger wasn't so easily mollified.

'I could give you plenty of reasons why . . .'

Jinx cut her off. The absolute last thing she wanted was to have any of those reasons aired publicly, and she knew that once Vivian got started, there'd be no stopping her. That kind of embarrassment Jinx didn't need and wouldn't have.

'Look, it just isn't that important,' she declared, giving her friend's arm a slight twist to ensure she got the message. 'The damage is done, and now that we've nearly got it cleaned up, I have to say it isn't all that much. Don't forget all this stuff has to be properly typed and collated later anyway. All we've lost is a bit of time, and it won't take me that long to sort the data out again.'

Vivian wasn't impressed, but Jinx persisted.

'Please. Can we just drop it? I know you're angry, Vivian, and so am I. But there's nothing to be gained by raising all sorts of ruckus over this. There's nothing anybody can prove, and believe me, it doesn't make that much difference anyway.'

It sounded stupid in her own ears, and Jinx knew that to Vivian it would be interpreted as taking Race's—and therefore Melissa's—side. But she really didn't care any more. All she wanted to do was put aside all the hassles and just get this voyage over with as soon as possible.

'You're the boss.' Vivian's acquiescence was grudging, and Jinx could only pray she'd stick with it. A blazing row with Melissa could only make things worse from her own point of view, especially with Morgan blindly taking the girl's side.

It was the final straw, she decided. When they arrived in Darwin she would be on the very first flight out. Race could keep his blonde and she, she hoped, might regain her shattered composure. The important thing now was to keep things peaceful and try to avoid both the captain and Melissa at all costs. Surely, she thought, that could be managed with only one more day to go.

The answer to that came all too quickly. Vivian, released and only barely compliant, slammed her way past Morgan and out of the galley, but Race didn't take the opportunity to leave himself.

'I'm really sorry about this,' he said. 'And I want you to know that I'll damned well find out the truth of what happened . . .'

'Don't bother! It just isn't *important*; can't you understand that?' Jinx raged. She was very closed to breaking now. She was alone with him yet again, and she didn't want to be alone with him, didn't want to have to look at him, to listen to him. She had to get away, and there was nowhere to go!

'It just . . . isn't . . . important!' she repeated, and turned away to finish picking up the scattered papers. 'Not important at all. So just *please* leave it.'

'You're sure?'

She didn't bother to reply, wasn't sure she dared. It wouldn't matter what was said now. He'd taken sides, and nothing was likely to alter the result. Best to just try and forget about the incident, although she'd make very, very certain it couldn't be repeated.

She continued her clean-up, head down and silent, until Race finally took the hint and left. Vivian returned only minutes later.

'What is the *matter* with you?' she demanded. 'Bad enough that you let that little bitch win in the bedroom, but do you have to give her a win here? This is your career we're talking about.'

Jinx didn't reply for a moment. How could she put into words that Melissa's win made her career irrelevant, that having lost Race, she didn't care about her career, didn't care about anything except getting off this damned boat and away from it, and him, and . . . everything?

'Look,' she said, 'it's happened and it's done, and nothing's going to change that. As for the rest—well, it doesn't matter all that much . . .'

'Doesn't matter? The bastard's treating you like . . . like . . .'

'Just like you warned me he would,' Jinx interjected. 'So I don't see why you're acting so surprised. And it really doesn't matter, so please stop being defensive on my behalf; I don't need it and I don't want it.'

Vivian stared at her, then shook her head sadly.

'All right,' she said. 'If that's what you want, then all right. Although *I* wouldn't let Melissa get away with *any* of it—just on principle. If I were you, I'd keelhaul her and then drop our beloved captain fair in the drink with her. Damn it! The whole thing stinks, and it makes me furious, mostly because I always thought better of Race Morgan than . . . than this!'

'It wouldn't be worth the trouble,' Jinx sighed. 'Not for me, at any rate. So let's just drop the subject, OK? I'll get started sorting this stuff out and you can start breakfast. I'm dying for a cup of coffee.'

Vivian accepted, but as she boiled the billy Jinx could hear her muttering about arsenic and keelhauling and various other threats of vengeance.

It would have been funny had it not been so tragic. Jinx found herself very glad she'd been wrong about Vivian in the beginning, and more glad she'd taken the time to know the tall redhead. Vivian made a good friend, and it seemed at the moment she certainly didn't need another enemy.

Breakfast, when it finally came, bordered on being sheer farce. Vivian slammed about the galley, scowling at everyone and all too clearly spoiling for a fight.

Jinx had contemplated missing the meal altogether. She thought Vivian might forget her good intentions if Melissa put a foot wrong while Jinx was present. Then she reconsidered, deciding that the same problem might be worse in her absence. Besides, she was ravenous.

Melissa didn't come for breakfast at all, but instead was seen heading for the afterdeck, and from the look on her face Jinx thought the vandalism must at least have been mentioned. Certainly the girl seemed subdued, but then, Jinx thought, she might just have had a busy night.

Race did come for breakfast, and somehow managed to convey the impression that all was normal, a difficult job when his plate was slammed down in front of him by a petulant Vivian, the bacon burnt, the eggs undercooked and the toast bordering on inedible.

Jinx couldn't bear to watch, but equally couldn't bear not to. Race struggled through, somehow, but she marvelled at his control while wondering why he would accept such treatment, and thought to remind Vivian later that it might be wise to tone down her protest gesture.

Vivian accepted Jinx's comment with little grace and absolutely no penitence.

'What's he going to do—sack me?' she laughed. 'The way our great Captain Morgan is going, he's lucky I feed him at all. And as for his little blonde girlfriend, she'd best go hungry till Darwin, if she knows what's good for her.'

'Oh, stop it!' snapped Jinx, annoyed now. 'You know very well Race could make things difficult for you with your own department, and if you keep pushing him, he very likely will. You'll get a splendid report from me, so don't go spoiling things just for the sake of being vindictive.'

Vivian's vividly obscene reply about what her department could do with Race Morgan's influence was surpassed only by the addition of what Race Morgan himself could do. Jinx listened to the tirade wide-eyed and with a certain admiration for such a skilled use of sailor's vocabulary.

No wonder Vivian's reputation outside work capabilities was so vivid! If I were Race, and I'd heard that little diatribe, she thought, I'd go hungry until Darwin myself.

As things turned out, nobody had to. Vivian, after spending most of the morning helping Jinx document the frozen specimens, returned to at least approximately her normal cheery disposition by lunchtime, and dinner survived also without incident.

Jinx stowed the papers away safely that night, and when they steamed into Darwin Harbour the next morning, there had been no repeat performances of vandalism or any other problems.

It took most of the morning, then, to arrange storage and shipment of the specimens and records. Jinx handled these details personally, and the chores were interspersed with useless telephone calls to Hobart.

Overall, a pretty subdued performance. Normally the end of a cruise would mean a bang-up party or expensive dinner where both boat and scientific crews could celebrate, but this time there was no interest in celebration.

Jinx, especially, was in no mood for such things. All she wanted to do was find out why she'd been pulled off the expedition and get away from Darwin and Race Morgan. Not even in that order, she thought at one point. The *why* could wait; getting out of Darwin couldn't.

Race and Melissa had, thank goodness, disappeared moments after their arrival at the wharf. Everyone else managed to keep busy with the unloading, but by noon there was just about nothing left to do, and it was clear they were getting impatient to be paid off and gone.

Jinx had managed to get a standby booking on a flight that very afternoon, but the first firm booking she could depend on was the next day. Vivian had offered her a place to stay the night, if that was required, and she'd gladly accepted. The sooner she got away from this boat, she thought, the better!

Race still wasn't back by noon, but Dick French and the rest of the crew weren't concerned. Having ascertained that there was to be no celebration, they gently wished Jinx farewell and then disappeared themselves, obviously unhappy with the way things had worked out, but pragmatic enough to realise it was too late now to change anything.

'See you next trip,' said Dick, giving her a swift hug before he departed. 'And stop worrying; whatever went wrong couldn't have been your fault.'

Jinx tried to make light of it all; nothing had been *his* fault either. 'Oh, I usually manage to live up to my name one way or another,' she joked. 'If I'm to come back again, I reckon I'll change it first.'

'Don't you dare,' he replied. 'That's as silly as the old tradition against having women aboard, which is also something I no longer believe in.'

Jinx noticed that he was looking not at her but at Vivian when he made that comment, and couldn't help wondering . . .

She'd been too embroiled in her own emotional difficulties during the voyage to really notice, but in retrospect it seemed Dick and Vivian had become closer than she might have thought. Noticing now that he didn't offer more than a casual farewell to the redhead before striding off down the wharf, Jinx thought she might well have missed the start of something important.

She hoped so; it would be nice to have *something* good come of the voyage.

Thoughts of that nature sustained her through the long flight home. Vivian had got her to the airport and her standby booking held good. There had been a twinge of conscience about not saying goodbye to Race Morgan, but they'd been able to catch Will Jacobs at home for a proper farewell, and Jinx thought that far more important.

The old captain was nearly recovered, and his warm reception was a highlight of an otherwise bleak day. 'I'll be fishing again in a week,' he'd said. 'Fit as a Mallee bull now.'

Jinx had suspected he was exaggerating, but he looked so much better, and so enthusiastic about returning to his beloved *Perfidy*, she could only agree with him.

'And the next trip will be better for that,' she had assured him. 'I missed you, you old goat, I really did.'

She would miss him too, she mused during the long flight. Because she had a horrible suspicion there might not *be* a next trip. As she had been unable to catch her boss by telephone, there was no hard evidence for her feelings, but instinct said there was more wrong than she could even suspect.

And besides, a return to Darwin, whether in six months or next year, would always hold the risk of meeting Race Morgan again. That, she could defintely do without!

By the time she reached Hobart, with Mount Wellington in a jaunty cap of crisp winter snow, Jinx was actually beginning to feel she had things under control. Her emotions were battered, but she would cope somehow. Easier here, at least, than in Darwin.

She went straight home from the airport, slept surprisingly well, and was in her office first thing next morning. Which was when things really fell apart!

CHAPTER NINE

'I HAVE TO SAY that I'm extremely disappointed in you.'

That was the first thing that the chief of the fisheries research division said when Jinx apprehensively entered his office.

He didn't wait for her to sit down; didn't, in fact, even offer her a seat. She had hardly closed the door to his office behind her when the scourging started.

But she was, at least, vaguely prepared. The typically vague, threatening comments of her immediate boss moments before had made it clear that the chief was very, very upset.

'The reputation of this division is extremely important,' he continued. 'I would have expected you to realise that and act accordingly. In fact I can't imagine whatever possessed you,' he went on.

It was clear she wasn't expected to answer the implied question, so she didn't bother. Instead, without invitation, she took a seat across the desk from the division chief and settled herself to wait out the storm.

It was her first one-to-one interview with the chief since she'd first been hired, but his reputation as a ruthless office politician was known throughout the division, and she had a fair idea what to expect.

'Can you imagine the political implications?' he asked then, still obviously not expecting a reply because he gave no time for one. 'The Northern Territory Fisheries *Minister* demanding explanations? From *my* Minister?'

Jinx shivered inwardly. This was worse—far worse—than she'd anticipated. Whatever was he on about, she was in deep trouble. The Minister had somehow become involved, which meant heads must roll, which meant *her* head.

For an instant, her mind blotted out the chief's voice as she idly wondered if Vivian might know of a job for her. Then she realised that would mean Darwin, and Darwin meant . . . no, she'd forget that avenue.

Her chief continued, saying nothing concrete in a barrage of words that went on and on and on.

Worse, most of it made no sense. He'd said nothing about the work she'd done; hadn't mentioned the engine breakdown, obviously hadn't read her cruise summary, since she hadn't written it yet. What was he on about?

After the fifth time he'd waffled on about the division's reputation and all these unspecified threats to it, Jinx's patience broke. After all, she thought, I'm obviously going to get the sack anyway; the least I can do is hurry things along a bit. And whatever else, I'm going to find out exactly *why* I'm being sacked.

'Chief,' she interjected, when next he paused for breath, 'I'm sorry, but I don't have the faintest idea what you're talking about. Do you suppose we could get a little specific here, like could you just tell me *exactly* what I'm supposed to have done?'

'I should have thought it was perfectly clear,' he replied with a scowl. And then, astonishingly, 'Or haven't you been listening to me?'

'You haven't said anything,' she replied flatly, and could have laughed at the expression on his face if only the matter weren't so serious.

'I've been talking about your disgraceful performance while in Nhulunbuy,' he shouted. Actually shouted! 'What did you think I was on about?'

Jinx sat in stunned silence, her mouth moving but nothing at all coming out. Her *disgraceful performance while in Nhulunbuy*? This didn't make any sense at all.

She finally managed to collect herself and looked up warily to meet the chief's beady, hostile glance. She took a deep breath, then said, 'I don't know what you're talking about.'

He was already practically foaming at the mouth and she had to raise her voice to talk over him, to hold his attention. 'To the best of my knowledge, absolutely nothing happened in Nhulunbuy involving me or my crew that could in any way have affected this division's reputation. Or my own, for that matter,' she added.

The chief seemed to have heard, seemed to have listened, but his reply made her wonder.

'Your reputation is the division's reputation when you're away on division business.'

Jinx fought back the urge to just get up and walk out. There was time yet for that; now she needed information!

'Damn it!' she cried. 'What am I supposed to have done?'

And when he began to prevaricate, she cut him off in mid-sentence, shouting him down. 'I want to know exactly, specifically, what I'm supposed to have *done*!' she yelled. 'Specifically! Who did I kill, who did I maim? What in God's name are you accusing me of—piracy or prostitution or what? *What?*'

To her surprise, the chief took her tantrum without blowing his own stack, but she could see her future with this division would be very short indeed.

'I am talking,' he said very slowly, 'about your atrocious behaviour during what has been described as a mobile drunken orgy through the suburbs of Nhulunbuy.'

'A what?' Jinx was open-mouthed with shock. She had done nothing to be ashamed of, except perhaps having a too-public nap. But a mobile, drunken orgy? 'You're talking about *my* behaviour, mine *personally*?' she asked at last. 'Not somebody in my crew?''

'You—personally!' That, at least, was clear.

'And may I enquire just who had accused me of . . . of whatever?'

'I don't know.'

Jinx couldn't control her astonishment, and even if she could have, she wouldn't have tried.

'You don't *know*? Do you mean to say you cut short my cruise, pulled me in here and tore strips off me for my *alleged* behaviour, and you don't even know who's made the accusations?'

The chief had the grace to look embarrassed—a least a little—but had the gall, the utter gall, to fall back into a typical public service defence.

'The Ministers have obviously . . .'

He got no further.

'Damn the Ministers!' cried Jinx, jumping to her feet and standing to the fullest of her never-tall-enough height. As she glared across the desk at him, it was tiny consolation to watch the chief shy back away from her fury. 'I want to know specific details . . . exactly what I'm supposed to have done . . . and with who—whom!—and I want to know *who said I did*!' she shouted. 'And I want to know *now*!'

'But I . . .' He was on the defensive now, and she did her best to keep him there.

'You don't know, do you?' she snarled. 'You're putting me through all this and you don't even know if it's true!'

'The Ministers . . .' He tried again, but Jinx was long past accepting that rubbish. All the emotional trauma of the last few days converged in a boiling cauldron of purest rage. Her frustration with this hopeless bureaucrat, her frustration with Race Morgan—especially Race Morgan—boiled over to emerge in scalding tears and an even more scalding tongue.

'You spineless, useless, cowardly excuse for a man!' she raged. 'How dare you try and do this to me?' The diatribe went on and on, rousting on the bureaucracy, on the male sex in general, and on the unfairness of it all.

It wasn't until exhaustion slowed her vitriolic tongue that Jinx realised she had been seeing through her tears a montage of her division chief and Captain Race Morgan, whose ice-green eyes seemed to loom out of nowhere, whose bright-toothed grin seemed to mock her betrayal, laugh at her hurt, scorn her feelings.

The realisation stopped her. She looked at the chief, wondering for an instant what he could possibly make of such an assault, and just as quickly deciding it couldn't matter less. She'd be fired now on general principle; the truth about Nhulunbuy was no longer relevant to the issue.

But it was to her, and she determined to find out the truth no matter what else. She would go to the Minister, if necessary . . . to the Prime Minister!

The chief's silence matched her own for what seemed like hours, but it was he who finally broke that silence with a surprising, amazing suggestion.

'I think you should take a day or two off,' he said. 'Then return and put together your cruise summary, get your bookwork in order. Perhaps by then I shall have been able to get to the bottom of this.'

Jinx could hardly believe it. Not fired . . . or at least not yet. And he was actually going to investigate? She could only imagine the trauma such a decision must be causing in his bureaucratic little brain. Not that she cared; what was important now was to find out who had started these vicious rumours, who was out to get her. As Vivian would have said, she wouldn't have to look far!

The knowledge that the matter was being investigated sustained Jinx through the next few days. She took the suggested day off, added the next, which was a Friday, and returned to work on Monday morning with high hopes of a resolution.

Her immediate superior was civil, but cool—and predictably enough made no mention of the accusations or what was being done about them.

The chief didn't show his face in the building all day, or at least he didn't come anywhere near Jinx's small office and laboratory. But the day could hardly have been considered wasted, because her specimens arrived from Darwin in excellent condition and she was almost too busy to care if she was being put on hold.

She was busy the next day too, and didn't get round to worrying too much about things until the telephone rang mid-afternoon and she was asked to accept a call from Darwin.

'What's all this rubbish about drunk and disorderly at Nhulunbuy?' Vivian, as usual, didn't beat about the bush; she got straight to the point without so much as a 'Hello, how are you?'

'I only wish I knew,' Jinx replied, and spent the next ten minutes relating her ordeal with the chief.

'You should have jumped over the desk and clobbered him,' laughed Vivian. 'Hit him with something long and pointed.'

'I thought about it, believe me,' said Jinx. 'But then I wouldn't have found out what was going on. Not that I have . . . yet. What do you know from your end?'

'Only that there's a sort of subtle enquiry going on, or maybe we should call it an inquisition. They got to everybody else on the scientific crew before me, but from what I hear, nobody, including me, was with you the entire evening of the party, so nobody could say very much.'

'That's right. The only ones I remember seeing for any amount of time were Race Morgan and his little blonde,' said Jinx, then thought again. 'Listen, can you somehow put whoever's interested on to . . . oh, let me think . . . Ted Mallanby and Rick . . . something. I can't remember his name, but Ted will know. They were with me almost the entire evening.'

'Will do. And Dick's got some contacts around Gove; we'll get on to them as well. But seriously, Jinx, it's got to be that damned Melissa who's behind this. You know it!'

'I don't know it, but I can't think of anybody else. I suppose with her father's influence she might have been able to pull the thing off. But it would mean he'd have been in it with her. No politician worth his salt would start a hare like this just to keep his daughter happy.'

'Not Stewart, that's for sure. Rumour has it he's as crooked as a dog's hind leg and he'll be in anything if the money's good enough. But this whole thing doesn't make much sense from that point of view. He'd surely get no mileage out of setting you up.'

'Melissa might have thought otherwise, although that still doesn't add up,' Jinx admitted, then related the viciousness of the attack on her the morning after the party.

'Vindictive little girl, isn't she?' Vivian commented. 'You dance with my man—I claw out your face. You were luckier than you know, I reckon.'

Jinx shivered at the memory. 'Yes, I suspect you're right, but that doesn't explain how she could put her father up to a blatant political shafting deal just to get revenge on *me*. And why bother? She got what she wanted anyway.'

'I'd reckon she set it up just after we left Gove. And at that precise time, she couldn't have known she was going to win, could she?'

'Oh, I don't know, said Jinx. 'There's no way to figure *what* she'd think, or even if she was involved, although I certainly can't think of anyone else with both motive and opportunity. And why her father should get involved . . . it's just ridiculous!'

'Ridiculous, maybe. But very angry-making too. She's quite conveniently dropped out of sight, which doesn't make it any easier, but she's got to turn up sooner or later, and when she does I might just go and talk to her by hand.'

Vivian sounded a bit too eager for Jinx's liking. 'Oh, please,' she begged. 'What we need is information . . . facts . . . not more vindictiveness. If we can prove it's a set-up and prove she or her father or whoever is behind it, then we can do something. Your going off half-cocked won't solve anything.'

'OK, but maybe you'll change your mind when I tell you the skipper's dropped out of sight too. Any bets on whether they're together or not?'

'I couldn't care less whether they are or not,' Jinx lied. 'Except I suppose that means he hasn't been questioned about the party either?'

'You got it in one! Not that it matters much, since we know whose side he's on, and it isn't yours. Not if he's hooked up with Melissa.'

'Even so, I doubt if he'd lie for her,' said Jinx, then paused a second in astonishment at realising she was *defending* Race Morgan. She covered up quickly. 'Besides, there were too many other people who had me in sight most of the evening. He couldn't cover that up, surely.'

'Who knows? The skipper is a law unto himself. Always has been, by his reputation. But then his reputation is far too good to account for Melissa bloody Stewart or any other part of this. On his reputation alone, Race Morgan wouldn't touch that bit of fluff with a forty-foot bargepole.'

But he has, thought Jinx. I've seen it with my own eyes. And she couldn't help but wonder what hold the Stewart family had over Race Morgan.

'Are you still there?' Vivian's voice seemed to come from a great distance, and Jinx realised she'd got lost in her own head, not for the first time where Race Morgan was concerned.

'Yes, I'm listening,' she said. 'I was just thinking of something else, that's all.' And even after Vivian had finally closed the conversation, she found herself wondering why she kept trying to make excuses for a man who had betrayed her so badly.

Such thoughts troubled her through the rest of the day, a day in which yet again she heard nothing from her own chief about the so-called investigation.

She was home, still mulling over her telephone conversation with Vivian, when her phone rang, and she picked it up to hear the rollicking bass voice of Captain Will Jacobs.

'I've just heard, or at least heard some of it,' he said, leaving her to wonder if all Territorians had such a forthright approach to telephone usage. 'I've got people checking, and we'll get to the bottom of this one way or the other, but I could use a bit more information.'

'So could I,' admitted Jinx. 'In fact, I'm sure you know more than I do, because I'm down here in Hobart and nobody is telling me anything at all.'

'Your chief wants to be knocked off for shark bait, the way I hear it. He wouldn't last a week up here.'

'He's the least of my problems,' said Jinx with a sigh. 'He wouldn't give his own mother a decent reference—not that she'd deserve one, having had him. But since I'll probably get the chop in the long run anyway, that doesn't really matter. I'd just like to know!'

'And you will. As soon as Race gets back, we'll sort out those politicians and bloody useless public servant types, you mark my words. A pox on the lot of them, I say.'

Jinx found her throat going tight. It was difficult to speak; equally so to hear past the sudden ringing in her ears.

'I think you're forgetting that the Captain is firmly in the other camp,' she reminded Will Jacobs softly. 'I don't see him doing much for . . .'

'If you'd believe that, you'll believe anything,' he interrupted. 'Fair dinkum . . . next you'll be trying to tell me politicians are honest and fishermen don't drink.'

'I'd hardly go that far,' she chuckled, 'but really . . .'

'Don't give me really; from the sound of it, you don't know the meaning of the word,' he growled. 'Now what I want you to do is just sit tight. Race and I will fix everything; you can depend on it.'

If only I could, she thought, staring at the suddenly dead telephone. Will Jacobs, with his usual abruptness, had hung up without even saying goodbye. And without, she suddenly realised, giving her the expected ribald progress report on his recovery.

She tried twice to phone him back, but got the engaged signal both times and finally gave it up as a bad job. He was probably, she realised, monopolising the Darwin telephone system with single-handed, full-steam-ahead directness.

The third call came while wintry Hobart still slept and dawn was hours away. Jinx struggled up from sleep to answer it, and was trying to shake some comprehension into her mind when she said hello.

'What the hell's happening? I've only just got back and Will's making about as much sense as a drunken deckhand!' said Race Morgan's gravelly voice.

She couldn't answer. The voice seemed to sear into her soul, ripping out memories she had buried beyond finding, knowing, surely, touching emotions she didn't want touched.

'Jinx! Damn it, answer me!'

It was too early. Too early and far, far too late. She stared numbly at the receiver, which crackled with his growling demands, for a moment. Then she hung up without a word and went back to bed.

The phone rang and rang, but she closed the bedroom door, put a pillow over her head, and managed to ignore it, though she never truly got back to sleep. Images and memories kept surging through her semi-conscious mind, all tropical, all sensuous, stirring. And all, she kept telling herself, false.

She got through the rest of the week without hearing any more from Darwin, and still without anything from her chief, who she now realised was deliberately avoiding her.

But on the bright side, she thought, she hadn't been sacked yet, nor shoved into a position from which she could resign with a clear conscience. And it would come to that; she knew it with every instinct she had. Indeed, she rather looked forward to the experience.

The weekend was not a success. She allowed herself to be talked into joining an office group going to the snow at Mount Field, did so even knowing one of the party was a man whom she had dated often in the past. There had been some romantic interest, most of it on his part, but prior to the Darwin trip she had been quite amenable to at least considering her own feelings in the matter.

But now . . . He was still likeable, still a pleasant, comfortable companion. But romance? Jinx found the mere thought depressing. He was, by comparisons she didn't choose to dwell upon, startlingly bland and insipid.

By the end of the weekend, angry with herself but unable to avoid the unavoidable, she had been forced to tell him he was wasting his time. Which had been accepted in a manner sufficiently insipid that she didn't feel all that bad, only angry.

Race Morgan, she felt, had much to answer for.

Monday morning's mail brought a new problem, and she spent much of the day pondering, wanting a way out of the situation but unsure if she could find one. This was much more difficult than the problem of the weekend, because here there were feelings involved that truly meant something.

The card was embossed, but simple. It invited her to the wedding of Captain Will Jacobs and Ms Bliss Watson. In Darwin, one week hence. Jinx stared at the card, closed her eyes against Will's handwritten PS, which was a simple and genuine 'Please!'

She wanted to go. She wanted in the worst way to show her support for the match, because her experiences with Bliss Watson told her it was a good match, good for old Will and obviously good for the woman who had been married to him before and now wanted a second try at taming the old outlaw.

But she knew without being told that this wedding would have too many ghosts, and Race Morgan would be chief among them. For Will not to invite his boss, his friend, would be too much to expect.

For Jinx to attend the wedding and manage to avoid Morgan was even more so too much. And she knew that seeing him, being forced to talk to him, to interact with him in any way, would be disastrous for her.

He would, obviously, bring his Melissa. That alone might be sufficient excuse for avoiding him. But no. She'd been to enough weddings in her young life to know that totally avoiding Race Morgan would be impossible. As would being polite to either him or his blonde companion.

Easy enough to avoid. She was under a cloud at work; there was heaps to do in finalising the data from her voyage; they wouldn't give her time off anyway.

'And who am I fooling?' she muttered to the preserved baby shark that swam in a jar of formalin on one corner of the desk. 'I mightn't *have* a job by next week. I might have all the time in the world by then.'

But how could she explain it to Will? She loved the old seaman, who in his way had made her northern trips so very, very special in the past. To miss his wedding—ignoring entirely the fact that she had obviously missed several in the past—would be sadder than she wanted to admit.

Jinx had seen the fear in him during the hospital visit.

She knew he was vulnerable, and he knew it. His heart was bad and there might be every chance that his time on this earth would be short. Dared she ignore this request? Dared she take the chance that it might be the last time she'd see him again?

'I've got to,' she told the baby shark. 'I'm too damned vulnerable myself.'

She went out and bought a gift, promising herself it would be in the morning mail with her apologies.

That evening she spent an hour carefully wrapping the gift—a splendid serving tray of Tasmanian black-hearth sassafras—and five hours futilely trying to compose the letter that would accompany it. Her kitchen was littered with half-completed, inadequate efforts when she finally gave up at midnight.

'I'll do it in the morning,' she said, staring into the mirror as she brushed her teeth, trying to ignore the hollowness round her eyes, the dark circles.

But morning made the job no easier. She ended up taking the parcel to work with her, half decided to try and buy a suitable card during her lunch-hour. Surely some professional card-writer could express the sentiments she found it impossible to put into words.

Jinx had barely reached her office, only just sat down at her cluttered desk, when the telephone rang, and she was too slow off the mark. Before she could tell the switchboard operator that no, she wouldn't take a call from Darwin, Vivian's voice was ringing in her ears.

'Did you get the parcel yet? I sent it priority paid; you should have it by now.'

'The mail's not here yet. What parcel?'

Then something went strange with the line, and all she got was a garbled, choppy mess that included a telephone number—which she wrote down immediately—and some words that mingled into 'paper . . . won't believe it . . .

. . . wrong about . . . paper . . .' and a final 'phone me later.'

Jinx stared at the silent telephone, damning her friend for being so impetuous. She glanced through the newspaper she'd picked up en route to work, but nothing caught her eye. There was the usual political rubbish, the usual carnage on the highways, but nothing that made any sense from the telephone call. Hardly surprising, she thought; news that might be important in Darwin, wouldn't generally rate a mention in the Hobart papers, and vice versa.

Jinx was still pondering the mysterious telephone call when the office messenger arrived with her mail, and the mystery—or at least part of it—was quickly solved. The priority-paid parcel, cylindrical and smothered in stamps, was the Darwin morning paper from the day before. And the main lead story was outlined by three colours of felt pen—not that she could have missed it anyway!

FISHING TYCOON NETS POLITICIAN

The headline was predictably twee. But the side-by-side pictures below it—photos of Race Morgan, Mel Stewart and the blonde beauty of Melissa Stewart were quite sufficient to grab Jinx's attention.

As did the story that followed. It was more than attention-grabbing; it was positively astonishing! Jinx skimmed the details, unable to believe what she was reading.

Charges involving graft and corruption had been laid against the Northern Territory Fisheries Minister and his daughter Melissa. The charges, very serious indeed, had resulted from a lengthy investigation by Captain Race Morgan, one of the Territory's foremost fishing magnates. Informed sources—this curiously underlined twice—said the final clue in the long investigation had come from quite unfounded allegations against a scientist doing research in the Arafura Sea earlier in the year.

After that, the details became less and less clear, as much

as anything because Jinx's vision had become curiously blurred and great droplets kept falling to stain the newsprint.

The corruption involved a confusing network of Taiwanese and Japanese interests, but centred on—to Jinx's astonishment—the black-tip shark industry. There weren't enough details to tell her exactly how her speciality had become the centrepiece of the scandal, nor how the investigation into the allegations against her, personally, had capped the overall investigation.

She sat and stared at the newspaper, her mind a muddle of contradictory emotion and feelings. None of it made any sense, and Vivian's curious and garbled telephone call didn't make anything clearer.

Jinx was flipping through her telephone file when there was a firm knock on her office door. Before she could speak, the door was flung open and her divisional chief entered the room as if he'd been pushed, his mouth open and words erupting at phenomenal speed. Words like 'sorry . . . apologies . . . abject apologies . . . investigation', but they meant nothing. Her every sense was tuned not to this prissy little bureaucrat, but to the tall dark-haired figure behind him, the ice-green eyes, the startlingly appropriate city suit, the sombre, brooding, threatening menace in his stance.

CHAPTER TEN

THE CHIEF'S voice wound down, perhaps because he was finished, perhaps because he had finally realised that neither Jinx nor Race Morgan was really listening.

Each was motionless, each silent. Their eyes were locked as Jinx sat immovable behind her desk and Race stood, arms folded, blocking the chief's escape as effectively as a locked door.

'Listen to him,' the voice rumbled, demanded. The chief hesitated, then ran through his dissertation again, citing the apologies, the investigation, the compensations that would be offered, his personal, abject apologies, the lot.

Jinx listened, or tried to. But none of it meant very much, not coming from this colourless, insignificant little man, not couched in bureaucratic nonsense as it was. She heard, but she didn't really listen. Or care.

And when the chief had finished, fading to a close much like a wind-up toy running down, the looming figure in the doorway spoke again.

'Now it's your turn. So tell him.' The voice was funereal, echoing hollowly in the suddenly silent room.

'Tell him? Tell him what?'

Jinx's own voice, by comparison, was hesitant, jittery. She was having trouble discerning reality. Was this really Race Morgan? This looming, piratical figure? Here . . . in Hobart?

'Tell him where he can *stick* his bloody job!' the dark voice spat, contempt wrinkling a sensuous upper lip across teeth that sparkled against Race's dark tan. 'And then hurry up and get your gear together; we've got a lot to do and a lot to talk about.'

Jinx stared at him, her chief an insignificant blur in her peripheral vision. Race's eyes flashed with fiery pride, with insistence. And his grin, his bearing, all told her without words why he was in Hobart. He'd come for her. There was a sense of sharing, a laughing sense of conspiracy in that grin, an invitation that was yet a command, and she knew there was no going back if she was foolish enough to ignore it.

Jinx rose from her chair, stood herself at attention and tried not quite successfully to smother the laughter that was suddenly bubbling inside her.

'Yes, *sir*!' she said with a snappy salute, then turned and gathered her handbag, her jacket and the still-wrapped gift for Will's wedding. Then she stalked round the desk and stopped squarely in front of the chief, who suddenly seemed to have shrunk, to have shrivelled until she could meet him eye to eye. She stared into his eyes, seeing totally for the first time the ineffectiveness, the fear.

She said nothing, merely stared for a moment, and then turned to Race, who hadn't moved, who still loomed in the doorway.

'He knows, sir,' she said with her own voice thick with contempt. 'I don't think he needs telling.'

'Right!' Morgan snapped in his most captainly voice. 'Let's cast off, then, shall we, first mate?' They strode off down the hall in tandem, having quietly closed Jinx's office door behind them, and actually made it to the first stairwell before Jinx erupted in a squeal of laughter and collapsed in Race's ready arms.

He held her while they both gasped and howled and quite effectively startled the one or two astonished staff members who passed them, until they could regain enough control to leave the building by the car park entrance.

'You have your car, I presume,' Race said then. 'I came

by cab, but I didn't have the driver wait.'

'Yes, sir,' Jinx told him with a grin. 'And where to, sir?'

He laughed. 'Well, it can't be my place—yet—so I guess it'll have to be yours, unless you prefer neutral ground.'

'My place it is, sir,' she said with another brisk salute, and joined his laughter as they marched through the car park to her car.

If she'd lived much farther from work, Jinx wasn't sure they would have survived the journey. Her inattention to traffic was disgraceful as they both tried to talk at once, alternatively dissolving in gales of laughter as one or the other recalled the chief's pathetic cave-in.

'I told him if I didn't get the whole damned apology routine, and get it perfectly, I'd drop him through a third-floor window, for starters,' Race chuckled.

'And what did he say? I'm surprised he didn't call the police or something.'

'Oh, he threatened to. Even threatened to call the Minister, but when I plunked the Minister's card down in front of him so he'd have the number, it slowed him up a bit,' Race told her. 'Then I got on to what Will Jacobs had planned for him, and I actually thought he was going to cry.' He sighed. 'Lord, but I don't know where they get these bureaucratic little nothings! It's no wonder the country's in a muddle. I actually felt guilty for taking advantage of him, towards the end.'

'He's going to be awfully angry when he gets over the shock,' said Jinx, narrowly managing to avoid a smaller car that had the temerity to be where it should have been.

Race recoiled from the near-miss, and muttered something beneath his breath. He at first refused to repeat himself, and when she insisted, admitted only that it was something rude about women drivers. Whereupon she swerved to the side of the road, stopped the car, and turned to glare at him, trying desperately to hide the laughter bubbling inside her.

'Where are we?' she demanded in her most commanding voice.

'Hobart.'

'And whose car is this?'

'Yours.'

'And does that not make *me* the captain?'

'Yes, ma'am,' he replied with suitable humility, waiting until she was back in the traffic before adding, 'But wait till I get you home.'

The game served them well until they reached Jinx's small house in an inner suburb. But once alone with Race, alone with him in her own house, on her own ground, she found it couldn't be sustained.

Fortunately he didn't try.

'There's a lot to be said, and I'd like to go first if you don't mind,' he said seriously. 'But could we maybe have some coffee as we talk? It's a long story.'

Jinx made the coffee, feeling more and more self-conscious as she did so, aware of his presence, suddenly aware of how she'd just chucked in her public service career for ever, peripherally aware of him moving around, seeing her own life-style for the first time.

The water took for ever to boil; finding that she had remembered how Race took his coffee was suddenly a jolt. She nearly spilled the tray as she moved into the small lounge room where he seemed gigantic, almost frightening.

But once he began talking, that gravelly voice now soft, intimate, she was immediately spellbound.

'First off, I have to tell you that I love you, that I'm in love with you, and that when we get back to Darwin there'll be more than one wedding to attend.'

Jinx could only listen. His words went round and round in her head, and she understood them and yet didn't. But they sounded right, felt right.

They stared at each other through the long silence, then Race cocked his head and said, 'Did you hear what I said?'

'Umm.'

His grunt then was singularly uninformative; he accepted her nod and continued.

'However, I have to say you caused me heaps of trouble during that voyage. First off, because I hadn't expected . . . well, you! Which is a pretty silly way of putting things, I suppose.'

'It is different, especially when I'm sure Will must have told you at least something about me.' Jinx was almost enjoying this. His profession of love was solid now. She was comfortable with it, or at least enough so as to want to hear the rest.

'He didn't tell me how beautiful you are. Well, he did, but one gets used to not quite believing Will. He exaggerates occasionally.'

'Always.'

'OK, damn it—always. And you might stop smirking; this is hard enough.'

'Yes, Captain,' in her most submissive voice. But little points of fire were laughing in her eyes, and Race could see them.

'Right. Well, as you must know by now, I was sticking pretty close to Stewart and his daughter, and Will's heart attack gave me a perfect opportunity to get over Gove way to do a bit of poking around. Which I did.'

'Yes,' said Jinx. 'You did . . . stick close, I mean.'

Which gained her a withering glance of exasperation and a sigh that bowed his head.

'Yes,' he admitted, 'I did.'

'Please go on, Captain.'

'I'm trying,' he snapped, and for an instant Jinx wondered if she wasn't pushing things a bit far. But on the basis of the day so far, could she do anything else?

'You were, as I recall, being "close" to something.' She had to smother her laughter as Race's scowl took on explosive proportions.

'By the time we left Gove I had it virtually wrapped up,' he said flatly. 'Although I wanted some more information from Melissa, which you made it damned difficult to get.'

'I what?' Jinx couldn't believe her ears. She hadn't done a single thing after leaving Gove that could lead to such an accusation. 'How dare you?'

Now it was his turn to smirk. 'Very easily, although I must admit it was my own fault. If I'd ignored you at the party, which I should have, things would have gone a lot easier. As it was . . .'

'As it was?'

'As it was, I didn't get very far at all. She might be young and vicious, but she isn't stupid. And once she'd figured out how I felt about you . . . well . . .'

'Oh,' said Jinx, warm inside at the implied compliment but bubbling with mischief at just the sound of Melissa's name. 'And how could she figure that out, I wonder? *I* certainly couldn't manage it. She must have been very, very clever.'

'Damned clever,' Race continued, ignoring the cattiness. 'In fact, I think it was she who planned most of the scam they were involved in, and when they got dropped in the . . . well, you know what . . . she turned on her dear old dad so quickly it would make your head swim.'

'What a clever little possum, smarmed Jinx, then jerked back in alarm as he came out of his chair in a single predatory bound and lifted her into his arms.

'You're not taking this seriously at all, so why should I?' he growled, capturing her eyes with his gaze, her mouth with his own. She was lifted clear of the floor, had the breath practically crushed from her as he kissed her, couldn't have resisted if she'd wanted to. And of course she didn't.

The kiss went on for ever, until, breathless, she was partially released—partially. Race's hands, so powerful and so gentle, still held her slender waist.

'You haven't finished your story,' she managed to gasp, mischief still alight in her eyes and now matched by equal mischief in his own.

'And I won't, until I've heard you say you agree to marry me,' he said. 'If you don't agree, you'll go to a spinster's grave never knowing what really happened.'

'I will not! And why a spinster's grave? Do you think you're the only fish in the sea, then, Captain Morgan?'

'For you—yes!' And his lips descended once again to seal his claim, to tantalise her, demanding a response.

'But once I've heard the rest I might not want to marry you, assuming I ever did,' she replied conquettishly—only to find her mouth leaping to meet his kiss, her fingers clasping behind his neck in a collar fit for a slave.

His fingers played sensuous music along her spine, then slid beneath her blouse to heighten the tune, lifting her to new sensation. The warmth of him poured through the flimsy fabric, flowing through to melt her insides.

'You will,' he whispered between kisses that grew increasingly ardent. 'Oh, yes, you will.'

Jinx abandoned herself, then. This was no longer a word game, but a game of a quite different sort. A game of touching, being touched, of nerve-endings being roused to unimaginable heights, of learning about him, about herself, about them, together.

Somehow they made it to the bedroom; somehow her clothing disappeared; somehow Race was with her, lips and fingers and body questing, exploring, asking, satisfying!

He took his time, bringing her from crest to crest, guiding her as surely as he might guide a favourite ship through the worst of storms. And when they finally joined, when their bodies and minds united to make the best of storms, it was a typhoon of wondrous, joyous madness.

It was much, much later, curled in the crook of his arm, one hand toying with the coils of hair on his muscular chest, that Jinx finally found herself able to return to his story.

Race rolled over to gaze down at her, then planted a gentle kiss on her swollen lips before grinning and renewing the account. His voice was soft, and she closed her eyes to listen.

'Nobody could have been more surprised than I was when the Stewarts showed up at our island,' he began. Jinx squirmed happily at the 'our'.

'I thought at first they'd caught me out, so I wasn't all that upset to find we'd been recalled, although I was mad as hell from your viewpoint,' he continued. 'But of course I couldn't say much, because there was that final perfect chance to get what I needed from Melissa.'

'What you needed . . . and did you?' Jinx asked without opening her eyes, but with fingernails gently scraping the message across his chest.

'Stop that! Of course I didn't. She was so full of hating you, for some reason, that I might as well have left her behind. It would have saved the awful mess she made of your notes, for one thing.'

'Oh,' said Jinx. 'So now you admit you *did* know it was her? How very interesting!' And her fingernails moved lower, dug just slightly deeper.

'Well, of course I knew,' he snapped, reaching down to grab at her dangerous hand. 'But I couldn't very well say so without giving the game away, could I?'

'You mean you didn't trust me?'

'Of course I did!' he shouted, once again grabbing at her hand. 'Now stop that, or there'll be no sense in marrying me!'

'I haven't said I would, if you remember.'

'I remember, and you did even if you think you didn't.

And you *will*,' he growled, rolling over to pin her down, his hand holding down one wrist, his body the other. 'Now do you want to hear the rest of this, or . . .'

Jinx was tempted, but allowed him to continue talking.

'I could have killed her. And I thought for a while that Vivian was going to kill both of us. Did you *see* that joke of a breakfast she tried to feed me? That is one dangerous woman; I hope Dick knows what he's letting himself in for.'

'Stop changing the subject,' said Jinx, secretly pleased at the knowledge. Vivian and Dick were good together, and would be.

'All right. So once we hit port, I had one last stab at getting the dope from Melissa, and although I wasn't really successful, I did get what I needed.'

'Oh, did you?' she purred, catlike.

'Stop that! Yes, I did, but not about your situation.'

'My situation?'

'The business of being called in early. There had to be something behind it, and I suspected from the start that Stewart had to be behind it. Or both Stewarts, really, though I didn't know then just how powerful an influence Melissa was. What did you do to her, anyway? She really hated you, you know, poisonously so!'

'Kicked her into a swimming pool, for one thing,' Jinx replied demurely. And took you, for another, she thought happily to herself, but said nothing.

'You should have gone in with her and finished the job,' Race replied bitterly. 'I tell you what—she'd be the nastiest piece of work I've come across in a long, long time.'

Jinx mumbled agreement through lips that were being thoroughly kissed, and when they'd finished, asked, 'But if you didn't get the information from her, then . . .'

'That's where the tale gets a bit tricky,' said Race with a sheepish grin. 'Stronger measures were called for, and I guess you'd have to say it was something of a team—or crew—effort.'

'I don't understand.'

'Well, we had enough to launch, or to have launched, the prosecutions you read about in the paper,' he said. 'But we decided it wasn't enough once we found your reputation was getting dragged through the mud. So there was a council of war held, and . . . well . . .'

'And?' Jinx shoved him off her and tried to sit up, but Race laughed and kissed her back into submission before continuing.

'We decided that since everything seemed to be being done at ministerial level, there had to be powerful political elements at work. Which of course meant Melissa's father, the Honourable Mel Stewart.'

'Who everybody thought had you firmly under his thumb,' Jinx prompted.

'As they were supposed to. And as *he* thought,' Race laughed. 'But even that wasn't enough to get the information we needed out of him. Because of course I didn't dare show enough power to drag it out of him, at that point.'

'But you must have done something,' Jinx prompted again. This was important! This was personal! If Mel Stewart had done her in, she wanted every detail. 'Tell me, for goodness' sake!'

Race had the good grace to look slightly sheepish. '*I* didn't do very much at all,' he admitted. 'You've got somebody else to thank for dragging out all the gory details, and in fact I still don't know exactly how he went about shafting you, although I can guess.'

'So what happened?' demanded Jinx, almost annoyed now. How could he leave her in such suspense?

Race looked down at her and laughed. 'You'll love it, I think,' he began. 'We sent Vivian after him . . . with Dick's permission, of course. She said it was like shooting fish in a barrel. Very slimy fish.'

'I . . . I . . .' Jinx couldn't find the words, and Race stepped in to save her the trouble.

'Apart from the obvious, she loved it,' he said. 'Said she hadn't had so much fun in years.'

'I owe her for that one,' said Jinx, saddened and yet overjoyed by the strength of a friendship that had started on the wrong foot and come so good.

'Well, you'll have three weddings, at the very least, to start paying,' Race said, bending to kiss her. 'Will's, hers, and ours! Which gives us a few days for you to show me Hobart, and then, with your permission, we're going home!'

'Yes, please,' cried Jinx as she moulded her body to his, moulded her very being to his. 'Oh, yes, please!'

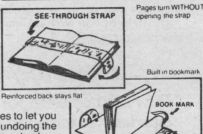

Six exciting series for you every month... from Harlequin

Harlequin Romance
The series that started it all

Tender, captivating and heartwarming...
love stories that sweep you off to faraway places
and delight you with the magic of love.

♦

Harlequin Presents

Powerful contemporary love
stories...as individual as the
women who read them

The No. 1 romance series...
exciting love stories for you, the woman of today...
a rare blend of passion and dramatic realism.

♦

Harlequin Superromance®
It's more than romance...
it's Harlequin Superromance

A sophisticated, contemporary romance-fiction
series, providing you with a longer,
more involving read...a richer mix of complex plots,
realism and adventure.

Harlequin
American Romance™
Harlequin celebrates the American woman...

...by offering you romance stories written about American women, by American women for American women. This series offers you contemporary romances uniquely North American in flavor and appeal.

◆

Harlequin Temptation™
Passionate stories for today's woman

An exciting series of sensual, mature stories of love...dilemmas, choices, resolutions... all contemporary issues dealt with in a true-to-life fashion by some of your favorite authors.

◆

Harlequin Intrigue™
Because romance can be quite an adventure

Harlequin Intrigue, an innovative series that blends the romance you expect... with the unexpected. Each story has an added element of intrigue that provides a new twist to the Harlequin tradition of romance excellence.

Harlequin Books®

PROD-A-2